MAN

Bartram—what a name! thought Regan scornfully when she heard that an unknown cousin was coming from Australia to stay at her parents' ranch in British Columbia. The man was bound to be as awful as his name. But Bart Kingman turned out to be handsome and forceful and Regan liked him very much. What a pity that he didn't like her one little bit!

Books you will enjoy
by ELIZABETH GRAHAM

RETURN TO SILVERCREEK

It was three years since Jan had parted in bitterness and misunderstanding from her husband Kyle Masters—and to this day he didn't know that she had had his son. Now circumstances had thrown them together, at his ranch in Vancouver, and at all costs she must prevent him learning the truth. For if Kyle did find out, Jan would lose her child . . .

NEW MAN AT CEDAR HILLS

'I don't need a man,' declared Abby Mackenzie—and indeed so far she was managing very well to run her ranch in Alberta and pay off her father's debts. But somehow, in spite of herself, she found she was relying more and more on the new man, Ben Franklin. But what was the good of falling in love with him, when he admitted that he loved his brother's wife?

MASON'S RIDGE

Greg Mason had married Cori simply for convenience: he wanted someone to look after his small nephew. He had said firmly that he wasn't interested in romantic love, so Cori had to accept the situation—but what about Greg's glamorous sister-in-law Marisa?

HEART OF THE EAGLE

For years Jinny had loved Bret Stafford—since long before her sister Lesli had walked out on him and married someone else. Now, Jinny was hardly able to believe that Bret had actually married her! It was even more difficult to believe when Lesli came back and it was obvious that Bret cared as much about her as ever . . .

MAN FROM DOWN UNDER

BY

ELIZABETH GRAHAM

MILLS & BOON LIMITED
17–19 FOLEY STREET
LONDON W1A 1DR

First published 1979
Australian copyright 1979
Philippine copyright 1979
This edition 1979

ISBN 0 263 72941 9

Set in Intertype Lectura 10 on 11 pt.

Made and printed in Great Britain by
Richard Clay (The Chaucer Press), Ltd., Bungay, Suffolk

CHAPTER ONE

IN retrospect, it seemed strange that Regan had had no inkling, no premonition, of the changes her life and character would undergo that morning in late April when her mother looked up from the letter in her hand to say calmly: 'We're going to have a visitor from Australia for the summer.'

'Australia?' Regan echoed, looking blankly at the older woman. 'But we don't know anybody in Australia. Why should anyone from there want to spend a summer here with us in Canada?'

'You forget my cousin Edna there, dear,' Hester Taylor said absently, addressing her next words to her husband at the other end of the oval dining room table. 'Phil, it's Edna's son. They're thinking of enlarging their cattle operation, and he wants to see how we go about things here. Edna says,' she glanced at the blue airmail paper in her hand, ' "You mentioned in your Christmas letter that you've had great success with your new cross breed, and Bartram is anxious to see for himself the results on your ranch with a view to enlarging our own operation." '

'*Bartram!*' Regan choked on her coffee, her face flushing to a uniform brick red. 'Heaven preserve us!'

'Regan, I wish we could see a little return in the way of manners from all those years we paid for you to go to that fancy private school!' her mother snapped in what Regan and her brother Russ had always called her schoolmarm manner. Hester Taylor had been just that in England before her marriage.

'I'm sorry, Mom,' Regan apologised, wiping her mouth with her napkin, her sherry-coloured eyes dancing with amusement. 'But even you have to admit that "Bartram" sounds just a bit like an undersized accountant with horn-rims!'

'The name happens to be a very proud one in the Kingman family,' Hester reproved. 'His father and grandfather, and possibly his great-grandfather, bore it before him.'

'That's enough now, Regan,' her father stalled the additional remark she was about to make, but the faint twinkle in his eyes as he frowned at her told Regan that he was almost as amused as she. His brow cleared when he turned to his wife. 'It's fine with me, honey, if you'd like to have him here. You know we'll do all we can to help him out.'

Hester smiled across at him, the flower-like beauty of her delicate skin and fair hair only slightly marred by the passage of time. 'I knew you'd say that, darling. I wouldn't normally want to worry you when you're not feeling well, but I've always felt just a little sorry for Edna and her family. Things haven't been easy for them. I know from her letters at Christmas every year. She always says how hard the living is there, it's such barren land where they are. Drought and desert, she wrote once.'

'Then how in the world do they support cows in a place like that?' Regan enquired, bored already with the subject of her distant Australian relatives.

'Well, they run some sheep as well, dear, so I suppose there would be enough grazing for cattle too,' her mother returned uncertainly, her face brightening again as she looked at her husband. 'Anyway, Phil, Bartram must have some idea of running a ranch—a station as they call it there—so he'll be of help to you now that you——'

'For Pete's sake, Hester, stop fussing!' he grumbled. 'I'm not ready for the last round-up yet!'

'Of course you're not,' Regan said lightly, rising and coming round the table to drop a kiss on her father's grey, but still thick, hair. 'But Mom's right—maybe our little cousin Bartram *can* make himself useful around the place. You know the doctor said you have to ease up a little.'

'Don't you start now, I've enough to contend with in your mother's direction!'

'It's just because we love you, sweetie,' she patted his shoulder gently and walked with her free, lithe stride to the door. 'I should be back for lunch, Mom,' she added before passing through it, 'I'm just going over to see Patty.'

'I'd have thought you and Patty would have seen more than enough of each other in Europe for the past six months,' her mother returned tartly, rising too and collecting up the used dishes although there was an abundance of house help to do just that. The ranch workers' wives were glad of extra pay on occasion.

'Patty has that last batch of pictures from our holiday to show me,' Regan called back. 'See you!'

She crossed the spacious hall of the two-storied rambling house, her brow creased between soft brown eyes when she went into the ground floor powder room and raked in a small side drawer of the vanity for the lipstick she used. She kept a supply of cosmetics in several parts of the house, finding it convenient not to have to run up the broad staircase and along one of the carpeted passages to her spacious room facing to the front of the house.

Patty was so fiercely independent that she had refused Regan's offer to pay for the developing of the last reel of film she had taken on their holiday together. So independent that she had insisted on keeping within her budget on their travels around Europe, which often meant their having to stay in student hostel type places here and there. Not that Regan had minded that too much—they had met a surprisingly wide variety of young people from far-flung countries and managed to have a wonderful time in spite of there being few of the luxuries Regan was accustomed to.

It was the comparatively small sum required to have the film developed that irked Regan now. Independence was fine, but sometimes Patty took it to the point of fanaticism. The two girls had been friends from their earliest years, and it had been only recently that Patty had become so conscious of the difference in their family finances. Patty had helped out in her father's small general store and service station for two years after leaving high school in order to pay for the European trip. But she had never resented Regan's expensive education at the exclusive girls' school on Vancouver Island, simply beaming her delight from shy blue eyes whenever Regan returned to the ranch for vacations.

The three of them—Regan, Patty and the loftily two years older Russ, Regan's brother—had spent long hours riding out to lakes in the vicinity of the ranch, swimming, having picnics and confiding with the confidence of youth their dreams for the future.

As Regan backed out the small red sports car her parents had given her for her eighteenth birthday, she reflected that only Russ was so far fulfilling his personally foretold destiny of becoming a knowledgeable rancher. He was now in his third and final year at agricultural school in Vancouver. Regan had always thought that a degree in agriculture and range management would be useless to him in view of the fact that he would one day inherit one of the most prosperous ranches in British Columbia, degree or not, but as usual Russ hadn't agreed with her. And, again as usual, neither had Patty.

This morning Regan found her friend in the small neat bungalow close to the store and service pumps which Patty's father ran with a minimum of help. Patty's mother had died when she was ten, and she was adept now at keeping house and cooking for her father and herself. Hester Taylor had done her best to supply substitute mothering for the small Patty, but when Regan went away to school there had been an inevitable drifting apart until the next vacation came around.

'I'm in the kitchen, Regan,' Patty called in answer to the other girl's distinctive knock at the front door.

'As if I wouldn't have known!' Regan grimaced, her nose wrinkling as the fragrance of newly baked bread filled her nostrils. 'I swear I'll get fat as a pig if I don't stop coming here on your bread baking days.'

'Oh, come off it!' Patty's light blue eyes, pointed up by the enveloping hyacinth blue of her apron, went appraisingly over Regan's streamlined leanness. 'You're like a greyhound; you'll never put on an extra ounce.'

'Hmm . . . sometimes I wish I could.' Regan reached for a still-warm loaf and a bread knife and cut off a hearty chunk of bread, spreading butter thickly on its finely textured surface. With a full mouth, she mumbled: 'I don't see too many spare ounces on your frame either, come to that.'

'That's because I watch every mouthful I eat,' Patty sighed, casting an envious glance at her friend. 'I'll put on some coffee and we can go see the pictures in the living room. If I stay out here much longer, I'll demolish a whole loaf and a pound of butter with no second thoughts!'

Ten minutes later they were sitting side by side on the sofa in the meticulously neat living room, gales of laughter shaking them as they relived the very last part of their holiday.

'Ah, Rome,' Regan sighed. 'Wasn't it wonderful, even though it was winter?' She peered more closely at the picture in her hand. 'Isn't that Humphrey Davidson? Must be, by the way he's glued to your side!'

'He only attached himself to me when he realised he couldn't beat off all the Adonises surrounding you,' reminded Patty drily, but Regan seemed not to hear as she bent even closer over the photograph.

'You know,' she looked up thoughtfully at last, 'he reminds me of somebody, but I'm darned if I can remember—oh, I know.' Her brow cleared and she chuckled wickedly. 'He looks just the way I imagine our visitor from Australia will look—all the way from his narrow shoulders to his thick glasses!'

'Humphrey may not have been an oil painting, but he was nice,' Patty returned quietly, then interest lightened her tone. 'Anyway, what visitor from Australia?'

Regan shrugged. 'Some poor relation of Mom's from the Outback. He's a rancher in a small way who has big ideas about running a herd the size of ours on the desert. He wants to come over here and see how we do things.'

'Well, he must think it's possible or he wouldn't be coming all this way—or spending all that money, if he's as poor as you think he is,' Patty pointed out reasonably. 'But why should you think he's like Humphrey? Have you seen a picture of him?'

Regan shook her head. 'Not that I remember. It's his name—can you imagine anyone with a name like *Bartram*? Bartram Kingman!'

Patty stared at her friend in level appraisal for a long moment.

'It *was* a little shortsighted of him not to object at birth to the name his parents chose for him,' she said drily. 'But maybe it's just as well, as he was fated to grow up to thick glasses and thin shoulders!'

'Oh, come on,' Regan said irritatedly. 'I don't know what's got into you lately, but you've lost your sense of humour all of a sudden.'

'I hope I never did have the type of humour that prejudged people and found them lacking,' Patty returned quietly, then injected a note of lightness into her voice. 'It would serve you right if he was six foot five and out of this world in the looks department, and you fell in love with him so hard you'd beg him to take you back to Australia with him!'

'Fat chance.' Regan rose and smoothed down the light brown top of her well-cut pants suit. 'I'd settle for Leo Shepherd first. At least he's only spending two years in Central America.'

'Do you think you'll go there to be with him?' Patty asked, following the taller girl to the screened front door.

'I don't know.' Regan lifted her shoulders in a shrug and let them drop again. 'I might. Leo's fun to be with.'

'In Vancouver, maybe. But you're talking about a primitive village cut off from civilisation as we know it—how's he going to amuse you there? Apart from the obvious way, of course.'

Regan ignored that.

'I could help him in his work.'

'And just what do you know about biology, apart from the couple of courses you took at school?'

'Oh, I could file his notes and have a drink ready for him when he gets back from a hot dusty day in the fields,' Regan quipped airily.

'I'd give you two days to tire of that pastime,' Patty snorted, 'and—well, say another couple of weeks to get over the novelty of sex without marriage. Leo did say he didn't want to get into the marriage bit, didn't he?'

Regan frowned. 'He'll be earning next to nothing while he's in Central America, so how can he consider marriage right now? Later, with that experience under his belt, we can——'

'I wouldn't count on it if I were you.' Patty's eyes softened. 'Look, Regan, you're no more the type to want that kind of relationship than I am. And apart from that, how would your family feel about it?'

'By family I presume you mean Russ?' Regan challenged waspishly, then felt ashamed as waves of embarrassed colour brought Patty's skin to awkward red. It was something they never talked about, never acknowledged, this painful love Patty bore for Regan's brother who, if he was aware of her at all, looked on her as just another sister, an appendage to Regan. Only Regan knew of Patty's silent agony when Russ succumbed to the charms of some local girl from time to time. Worse still was the uncertainty of knowing how many city girls were chasing his laughing good looks in Vancouver.

'I meant your mother and father,' Patty got out eventually, the soft lines of her mouth uncharacteristically firm.

'I'm sorry, Patty,' Regan apologised remorsefully, then covered her embarrassment with a light laugh. 'What Mom and Dad don't see won't hurt them!'

But driving away five minutes later in her red car, she told herself that Patty was right. Her parents would never understand the new morality that said two people could have a meaningful relationship without benefit of marriage certificate. No matter how precarious Leo's budding career, their advice would be to marry and work towards a more secure future, as they had.

But that wasn't Leo's thinking at all. Regan's heart changed to a higher gear when she thought of his dark good looks, the chiselled perfection of nose and mouth and chin. That she was not the only girl whose pulses leapt at thought of him was no deterrent in her eyes. The envy of other girls just added to his attraction for Regan.

She had met him at the home of a school friend in Vancouver where she had stayed for a few weeks. He was Carol Shepherd's brother, as popular with girls as Regan was with men. It had seemed inevitable that they should gravitate together, king and queen of the heart stakes in their group. Leo had visited the ranch a couple of times, and Regan had spent another three weeks at the family's spacious but unpretentious house in Vancouver, falling lightly in love with Leo's attentive pursuit. Or was it heavily? The truth was that she just didn't know if her feelings ran deep enough to enable her to toss off the opinion of her parents if they should find out that her projected trip to Central America was not for completely altruistic motives. While reserved in their judgment of Leo, they could nevertheless understand Regan's wish to help those less fortunate than herself.

Now Regan frowned. Leo had recently qualified as a plant biologist and now he had been offered the post of assistant on an international team of researchers. The salary would be infinitesimal, but the experience invaluable in his future career. Regan had nothing to offer undeveloped peoples in the way of skills. Oh, she wanted to help, but that wasn't enough. If she was a nurse, or a teacher, or a doctor, she could fill some necessary niche, but as it was, she was qualified only to be the mistress, more or less, of a junior member of an important international team.

Regan ran the car into the garage beside the main house and cut off the engine decisively, reflecting sourly that she wasn't even qualified in the field of being anybody's mistress either. As she walked to the house, an imaginary interview took place in her mind.

'What experience have you had in a similar position, Miss Taylor?'

'Experience? Well, none, actually.'

'And what makes you think you'll be right for this kind of work?'

'Well, I have all the normal responses when I'm kissed, and I like being kissed . . .'

'You feel that's enough for a position such as this, with possible deepened commitment in the future?'

'Let the future take care of itself! Anyway, how can I tell if I'll want a deeper commitment until I've tried it for a while?'

'That's just my point, Miss Taylor. You should have absolutely no doubts before embarking on such a career. Perhaps it would be better if you gave the matter considerably more thought.'

Grimacing mockingly at her own fanciful turn of mind, Regan entered the broad front door set at the back of a wide airy porch. For all her meditating, she was still no closer to coming to a decision about Leo and Central America. Which was ridiculous in this day and age of free choice of life style for women.

Sighing, she entered the dining room on the weak resolve to let things slide until Leo's visit three weeks hence. Surely it would be easier to decide when he was actually there, holding her in his arms and kissing her with practised skill.

The three weeks until Leo's visit passed uneventfully apart from a small flurry when another letter came from Australia in answer to the one Hester Taylor wrote welcoming Bartram Kingman. This time, the missive was in Bartram's own hand, and Regan reflected idly as her eyes went over the bold, unmistakably masculine script that readers of character by handwriting would have been badly foxed by Bartram Kingman's.

The letter stated offhandedly that the writer would arrive as close as possible to the twenty-fifth of May after taking a look at stock breeding farms on Vancouver Island. His thanks for the Taylors' willingness to accommodate him were no more than polite.

'I wish he'd given us some kind of idea about when his plane gets in from Australia,' Hester worried. 'Russ could have met him and taken him to the apartment for a night or two. He'll no doubt want to see something of Vancouver while he's here.'

She referred to the spacious two-bedroom apartment rented on a family basis, although normally Russ was its sole occupant. However, it served as a home base for the occasional visits the older Taylors made to the city, and for Regan when she felt the need for a break from the ranch.

'It sounds as if he knows what he's doing,' Regan remarked drily, tossing the letter back to her mother's place at the table. A gleam of mischief lit her sparkling brown eyes. 'Anyway, maybe our little Bartram is a dark horse on the sly. He's not married, is he? Maybe he's bringing a girlfriend with him!'

Hester's brow creased still further. 'Do you really think so, dear? No,' she shook her head, 'Edna would have told me if I was to expect more than just Bartram. Besides,' she added severely, 'I'm sure that no boy of Edna's would ever travel on the loose with a girl not his wife.'

'Boy!' Regan said explosively. 'He's older than Russ, isn't he?'

'Let me see now ... hmm ... Edna's quite a few years older than me, and she was married six years before me ... Bartram was born within a year ...' By an involved series of calculations, she came up a moment later with a triumphant: 'Bartram must be thirty now.'

'Not so sweet thirty and never been kissed,' Regan misquoted lightly, getting to her feet and giving her startled mother an impulsive hug before going to the door, where she bumped into her father.

'Who's thirty and never been kissed?' he enquired mildly, his eyes lighting up as usual when he looked into the deep sparkle of his daughter's. 'Nobody around here, I'll guarantee!'

'Oh, Phil, I wish you'd speak to her,' Hester complained, levelling a severe look at Regan. 'I won't have her upsetting Bartram with her teasing while he's here. Edna would never forgive me if he went home and told her we'd been inhospitable and rude.'

'You heard your mother, chicken,' he reprimanded dutifully, then chuckled as he patted Regan's cheek. 'Whatever he's like, we're going to do our best to show him what real Canadian hospitality's like!'

'All right, Dad, I'll be good and very, very nice to little Cousin Bartram.'

'The relationship is a lot more distant than that,' Hester said, her voice conveying her disapproval of her husband's method of correcting their daughter. 'Edna is only second cousin to me, so Bartram is hardly related to you at all!'

'Praise be!' Regan uttered in a heartfelt undertone and heard her father call after her departing figure.

'When are you going to see to that correspondence piling up in the office?'

In a haphazard way, Regan had taken over much of the inevitable paperwork, a confining occupation which her father hated even more than she did. Since the doctor had told them of the weakened state of his heart, however, Regan had gradually eased that part of his burden from him.

'As soon as I get back from town,' she called back. 'I want to get it all up to date before Leo gets here.'

There was a resounding silence from the room behind

her, and she could imagine the significant glances being exchanged between her parents. They didn't really like Leo, although they were hospitality itself on his visits to the ranch. It was almost as if they sensed that his intentions were not the honourable ones they wanted for their daughter from a man who supposedly loved her. She knew their thinking. If he really loved her, why did he hesitate to make their commitment to each other lasting and deep? Sighing, she reminded herself that they were hopelessly old-fashioned and would never understand the up-and-coming generation.

As it happened, Leo's week-long visit turned out to be a bigger trial for her than for her parents. Time was running short, he told her. He was leaving for Central America in two weeks' time, and he wanted her answer before he left. An answer Regan was still not able to give him.

'It's such a long way away,' she tried to explain her misgivings, 'and I'd never forgive myself if—if something happened to Dad and I wasn't here.'

'Oh, come on, Regan,' he burst out impatiently. They were standing on the verandah that evening, looking out to the lake which shimmered gently under the cool rays of a young moon. Now Leo turned and gripped her arms. 'Nothing's going to happen to your father—and if it did, you could be back here in no time by air.' He shook her slightly, a dark strand of his hair falling attractively over his brow. 'You can't stay wrapped up in the cocoon of your family for ever, Regan. You have to make the break some time, and it might as well be now.'

Then his well-cut lips were at her ear, his arms intimately familiar round her. 'You know I'm crazy about you, honey. Give me the chance to show you how much.'

Oddly, the feel of his lips on hers failed to stir her this time. Reaction to the weeks of indecision, she told herself numbly as she tried to force a response, but it was with relief that she heard her mother's voice behind them.

'Would you two like to have your coffee out here?'

Regan knew that quality in her mother's voice—overlying politeness underlaid with a hint of pure steel. Leo sensed it too, and muttered an oath as he released Regan.

Matters didn't improve between them, and when Regan drove him into the airport at Kamloops, the southern cattle centre for British Columbia, she had still given him no definite answer.

Pausing at the head of a column of traffic until the light changed to green, Regan was taken by surprise when Leo muttered: 'What does it take to make up your mind?' and grasped her chin in his fingers, turning her mouth to the swift descent of his.

Her foot slipped from the brake pedal and the car began to edge forward. Panicking, she jerked away from Leo, her foot coming to rest on the accelerator so that the car leapt forward. At the same time as she took in the frail-looking figure of an elderly woman crossing in front of them a blurred male figure came from the side and hustled the old lady beyond reach of the threatening bumper. Stamping automatically on the brake pedal, Regan brought the car to a shuddering stop and looked with wide-eyed fearfulness at the tiny woman sheltered protectively by a long grey-suited arm.

The man's blond head turned and contempt edged the bronzed outlines of his lean face and flickered in the light-coloured eyes he raked over Regan and her companion. She gazed mesmerised at the movement of taut lips, the words inaudible in the sudden beeps from traffic behind as the lights changed colour. It wasn't hard, though, to guess what the tall stranger was saying.

Shakily, she put the car into motion and left the crossing, glancing quickly into the rear view mirror to see that the oddly assorted couple had reached the further sidewalk and that the elderly woman was looking up at the man with adoring gratefulness. But his head was still turned in the direction of Regan's car, and she knew with a strange shiver that he would not easily forget her or her car. And that made them equal. She would never, ever, forget the contemptuous disdain in his look.

'Why did you do that?' she hissed to Leo, waves of humiliation rolling over her in the knowledge that the stranger must have known the reason for her negligence at the wheel.

'How did I know you'd take your foot off the brake?' Leo returned savagely. 'What does it matter, anyway? The old lady's all right, and you'll never see the fellow again.'

Regan gritted her teeth and drove with slow caution to the airport, heaving an inner sigh of relief when Leo's plane was a mere speck in the sky. Sensing her agitated state of mind, he had wisely refrained from pressing her further about Central America, contenting himself with saying that he would phone her next day from Vancouver.

Knowing that she was in no fit state to drive the thirty-odd miles home, Regan decided to do a little shopping and have coffee somewhere first. So it was a good two hours later when she swung away on to the less travelled highway and headed for home.

She had bought a gaily coloured silk square for her mother, and a new hide billfold for her father, remembering his plaint of a few days before that his old one was in tatters.

Peace-offerings? For what? To assuage her guilt at having contemplated doing something that would have broken their hearts if they had known? With a lightheaded sense of relief, she realised that contemplation was as far as she would ever have gone in the matter of becoming Leo's mistress. Whether the afternoon incident, with his callous disregard for the elderly woman, or his equally callous inability to understand her parents' point of view, was responsible for the sudden decision of her heart, she neither knew nor cared.

Happier than she had been for weeks, she garaged her car and walked towards the house, finding fresh beauty in the pretty setting of her home with its rolling lawns sweeping down to the narrow sand strip bordering the small lake which in turn led to endless miles of sage-covered hills and stark rock outcroppings that constituted her father's property. In a day or two, the memory of that afternoon's near-accident would fade and grow less fearsome . . . as would the tall, lithe figure of the stranger with his contempt-filled eyes.

The unfamiliar rented car she had seen parked close to the garages meant nothing to her. It would be more unusual for the Taylors to have a day, at this time of the year, without someone or other dropping by. So it was no surprise to hear her mother call as Regan let the screened front door bang behind her:

'We're in the living room, Regan. Come and meet our visitor!'

There was a note hard to pin down in her mother's voice. Glee? Satisfaction? Gentle revenge? Perhaps it was a mixture of all three, but Regan didn't stop to analyse it then. Smiling, the gold of her expertly cut pants suit casting a sunny glow upward to her skin, she entered the spacious but homely living room.

Her father was there in his customary place in the winged armchair close to the empty fireplace, her mother opposite in the low tub chair she favoured. A man sat on the sofa facing the fireplace. Tall, because his wide shoulders came high above the sofa back. Blond, because the sun shafted through the room to where he sat, casting a god-like halo round his head. Strangely familiar, because . . .

'This is Regan,' her mother was saying, as if they had been awaiting her coming.

Slowly the tall figure unfolded itself from the sofa and turned to face her. Her knees weakened and threatened to collapse beneath her. Dear God, why had he come here? Had he followed her, intent on making her hear the words that had been inaudible to her at the traffic crossing? But he couldn't have done that, he was already here when she arrived. Had he asked someone who she was, someone who knew her?

Then as her stricken eyes looked into the shocked lightness of his, she knew that this meeting was as much a surprise to him as to her. Why, then——?

'Regan,' her mother supplied with the air of a conjuror producing a particularly desirable rabbit from his top hat, 'this is cousin Edna's son, Bartram.'

CHAPTER TWO

THE blond giant recovered his aplomb far more quickly than Regan. While her mouth still hung open unattractively, he rounded the sofa and came towards her with a long-legged stride, opening his grey-suited arms to embrace her.

The arms were hard, muscled, speaking of long hours of physical labour over the years; the cheek he laid against hers was smooth-shaven but tough; his brushing lips at her temple firm with a hint of softness. Then he was holding her away from him and looking down at her with a steely mockery in his eyes.

'Well, Regan,' he drawled in the unfamiliar accent that brought a gust of Australia into the room, 'for a moment there I thought I recognised you. But that can't be so, can it?'

His eyes were more green than blue, like the mingled reflection of sky and pines in deep lake water. Ice lurked in their green depths, too, and Regan closed her mouth and regarded him warily. Her own words came back to haunt her. 'Not so sweet thirty, and never been kissed.' In the space of a second and without the blink of an eye, she reversed that decision. This man had been kissed by—and had kissed—many women in his time. The only marvel to her stunned brain was that he had remained unmarried.

'I—er—it seems unlikely that we've met,' she offered tentatively to the gleam of amusement now lurking in his eyes. It was as if he knew that she was calculating how possible it was that he would tell her parents about the near-accident and its cause.

'Most unlikely,' he agreed gravely, and dropped his arms from her waist. She followed him to the fireplace, breathing a relieved sigh that he had apparently dropped the subject of recognising her.

He waited politely until she had seated herself at one end of the sofa, then took his own place at the other end, unbuttoning his jacket over a pale grey silk shirt as he did so.

'You've been such a long time, dear,' her mother probed. 'Was Leo's plane late in taking off?'

'No—no, I decided to do a little shopping before I came back. Oh, that reminds me . . .' Regan leapt to her feet again and went to the hall table where she had left her packages. Somehow she had a feeling of constraint when she returned and dropped the respective packets on her parents' knees.

Under cover of their delighted expressions of pleased surprise, Regan glanced at the Australian and was shocked to find his eyes on her with an expression of disdain to equal and surpass his contemptuous look at the traffic crossing. How could he know, as the eyes seemed to tell her, that the gifts were meant as a propitiatory gesture against a sin, in her parents' eyes, which she had contemplated but not committed?

'Look at this, Hester, it even has my initials on it,' Regan's father held up the silvered initials on black leather and turned to his daughter. 'I didn't mean that you should go right out and buy me a new wallet when I complained about the old one, honey.'

'You know me, sweetie,' Regan returned lightly, perching on the arm of his chair and dropping a quick kiss on top of his head, 'if I'd thought you meant that, I'd have never bought you a new one.'

'That's for sure,' he chuckled, looking up at her fondly. 'Thank you, honey.'

As she slipped back to her corner of the sofa, the Australian drawl came again.

'Well, I won't gild the lily right now, but when I've done some unpacking there's a whole pile of presents Mother's sent to all of you. Every time I go looking for a clean shirt or socks, all I can find is parcels labelled "To dear Regan" or some such.'

While her parents laughed indulgently, Regan caught the level look he directed at her. Really, was he going to hold it against her for the rest of his stay that she had almost run down an elderly woman? As if by that piece of negligence she had forfeited the privilege of being addressed as his mother's 'dear Regan!' Her colour heightened, she returned his gaze and determined that as soon as she could get him alone she would set him right on a point or two.

'I so wish your mother had been able to come with you, Bartram,' Hester sighed. 'I haven't seen her since she went to Australia from England to marry your father. It seemed such a big undertaking in those days, to cross the world for love.'

'I don't think she's ever regretted it,' he said quietly. 'Not from the way she still misses Dad around the place. I did everything but get down on my knees to beg her to come with me, but she wouldn't be persuaded, much as she'd have liked to come.' He gave an affectionate laugh. 'I reckon she thinks the homestead would fall to pieces if she wasn't there to hold things together.'

'That could raise a peck of trouble when you marry, son, and want to install your wife in her rightful place,' Phil said bluntly, surprising Regan with his speedy acceptance of his wife's distant relative.

'I anticipate a problem or two,' Bartram acknowledged with a wry smile, revealing a bare glimpse of strong, even teeth, 'but nothing that can't be worked out if everyone's sensible.'

'Women seldom are in situations like that,' Phil grunted, and avoided his wife's kindling eye. 'Who's running things for you while you're away?'

'My younger brother, Jim. He hasn't shown too much interest in the place lately, so I thought it might do him good to get the feel of some responsibility.'

'And then there's your younger still sister, Victoria, isn't there?' Hester put in.

'Yes. Vicky's travelling in Europe at the moment with—um—a friend.'

Regan glanced swiftly at his suddenly shuttered expression. Did that hesitation over the word 'friend' mean that his sister was travelling with a man? His sudden withdrawal could easily be construed as disapproval, and Regan felt a stab of irritation at his high-handed assumption of authority over those in his sphere of living. First his brother, who had evidently knuckled down under Bartram's thrusting of unwanted responsibility on him, and now his sister.

'You must have a prosperous ranch if you can afford all these jaunts around the world,' she remarked tartly.

'*Regan!* Watch your manners!' her mother told her, vexed.

Bartram seemed undisturbed. 'That's all right, Aunt Hester.' Turning to Regan, he added impersonally: 'We call it a station, not a ranch, and yes, Rowanlee takes care of most of our needs. However, Vicky's a very talented interior decorator and can well afford this trip herself. It's what you might call a pre-wedding trip,' he explained, his mouth closing round the words as if they displeased him.

So Vicky was defying her brother's old-fashioned ideas and anticipating her wedding vows with the man she was travelling with! Good for her, Regan thought, admiring the unknown Vicky for going against this man who, she could see, could be a pretty formidable opponent.

'I'd like to meet Vicky,' she said, 'she sounds like my kind of girl.'

'Oh?' The fair, yet definite, line of his brows rose a fraction. 'Are you into interior decorating or something similar yourself?'

'No, I—no,' Regan denied, resenting the faintly sardonic cast of his eyes, irritated at her mother's quick defence.

'Regan hasn't made up her mind what she wants to do yet,' Hester put in. 'Of course, she's lucky in that there's no need for her to earn her living, though I'd always hoped——'

'Teaching might have been your thing, Mom, but it doesn't appeal to me one bit.'

'What does appeal to you?' Bartram asked, his expression veiled as he looked at her.

Phil snorted and looked with baffled affection at his daughter. 'Men—if the constant line-up around this house is any indication!'

'Really?' the younger man murmured, his brows rising further in an expression of puzzlement as if he, personally, found this unbelievable. 'I'd hardly have thought anyone could make a career out of the opposite sex, but maybe things are different here. I firmly believe that young people should have something worthwhile to occupy them—otherwise they're apt to get into mischief.' He looked at Regan with this last remark, and she knew he was referring to her 'mischief' of almost running over an old woman.

Her hackles rose and she snapped without thinking: 'Well, it might interest you to know, *Bartram*'—she stressed his name as insultingly as she could, 'that I'm considering going to Central America to help a research team there.'

'Regan!' her mother gasped, glancing quickly at her husband's astounded face. 'How can you possibly do that? You can't do anything to assist a team of scientists!'

'Oh, I don't know,' the lazy drawl came again, as if its owner had already carved a niche in the family circle. 'If it's a really remote spot, Regan's talents could shine there!'

Two spots of rage highlighted Regan's cheeks as she glared back at him, unable to speak for her anger.

'You're not really thinking of going there with Leo, are you, Regan?' her father's quiet question came, making her draw a shuddering breath and hasten to soothe the stunned hurt from his eyes.

'I've told Leo I'll think about it, that's all, Dad,' she said steadily.

'But there isn't a job you could do there, is there?'

'Well,' she hesitated awkwardly, conscious of Bartram's enigmatic gaze on her, 'I can take the paperwork off their shoulders—I've seen to the ranch records for quite a while now.' Her voice faltered, then she cried: 'I'd just like to do something worthwhile, Dad, for people who haven't been as lucky as me.'

'I'm sure the natives would be most happy to have all that paperwork taken off their shoulders,' Bartram put in drily.

'Oooh! . . .' Regan's eyes blazed as she turned on him, and Hester intervened hurriedly.

'Heavens, Bartram, I don't know what you must be thinking of us! We haven't even offered you a drink yet. What will you have?'

'Beer's fine, Aunt Hester, if you have it.'

'Yes, we have.' Hester turned to Phil. 'Will you have your brandy now, darling?'

'Yes, maybe I will,' he said heavily, his face pale though he gave Bartram a wry smile. 'I'm allowed one before dinner —had a little trouble with my heart.'

'Oh? I'm sorry to hear that. I suppose you can't do as much around the place as you used to.'

'No,' Phil said regretfully. 'That dratted doctor tells me I have to sit around the house like an old woman most of the time. It's not easy to keep on top of things right now with Russ being away at agricultural school. He finishes this summer, though.'

'Well, if there's anything I can do to help while I'm here, just shout out.'

'Thanks, son, I might do that . . .'

Regan followed her mother out of the room and into the big kitchen at the rear of the house, her seething emotions showing plainly on her face.

Martha, the cook-housekeeper who had been with the family since before Regan's birth and therefore considered herself one of them, mixed pastry at a huge central table. Her once black hair was now a not too tidy iron grey sheath round her plump features. She looked up with her dark button eyes when mother and daughter came in.

'Good-looking fellow, your cousin, Regan, huh?'

'I hardly noticed,' Regan replied coldly. 'All I did notice was his colossal conceit, his arrogance and his . . . his . . .'

'Stop that this minute, Regan!' her mother snapped with an anger unusual for her. 'You've been unspeakably rude to anyone who is a guest in this house, let alone that he's my cousin's son! Bartram is a fine, upstanding young man and I can only wish there were more like him around today.'

'But he's so overbearing! From the sounds of it, he rules them all with an iron hand—except Aunt Edna.'

Hester reached into the big fridge and extracted a bottle of beer from its depths. 'If he's a little forceful it's because he's had to be. Goodness knows it couldn't have been easy for him to take on the responsibility of a family and the ranch—station—when his father died. Especially as it seems not to be a very prosperous one.'

'That suit he's wearing wasn't made for a poor man!' Regan remarked waspishly. 'And how come he can afford to come over here on an extended vacation?'

'He told us before you came in that it's his first long trip away from the ra—station in years. Now, I want you to take this in to him, with a glass, and act as if you're pleased to have him here.'

Regan gaped stupidly after her mother as she swept out, hardly hearing Martha's deep chuckle.

'Poor or not, honey, he's a fine hunk of man! Anyway, cold cash doesn't do much to warm a woman's bed in winter.'

'You don't know what you're talking about,' Regan loftily told the unmarried housekeeper.

'Maybe,' the older woman retorted cheerfully, 'but at least I can recognise a real man when I see one. This one's a big improvement on the one who just left.'

Fuming impotently, Regan banged out of the kitchen and went back to the living room, where she noted that Bartram had moved into her place on the sofa so that he could talk more comfortably to her father. He had taken off his jacket, too, and her eyes were drawn reluctantly to the smooth ripple of muscles across his shoulders under the thin grey shirt as he leaned forward, elbows on knees, to tell her father about his visit to Vancouver Island's breeding farms.

'Thanks, Regan,' he paused momentarily to say as she placed bottle and glass on the side table at his left elbow, then went on: 'I'd thought I might have to go to Europe to get what I'm looking for, but after seeing what they've got there, and hoping to pick your brains here, there might be no need for that.'

Her father looked more vitally alive than he had for a long time, Regan noticed as she slipped into the place Bartram had vacated near her mother. And it wasn't just because of the careful measure of brandy he held in his hand, she knew. Only Russ, these days, came near to approximating that degree of interest.

She looked speculatively at what she could see of Bartram Kingman. The hands slowly pouring liquid from bottle to glass were big but not ungainly, having a kind of natural workmanlike grace about them. Long, powerful thighs strained the light grey worsted of his trousers and led to a length of calf and feet encased in large sized black polished shoes. Her eyes rose to the wide expanse of chest and bronze throat above knotted tie in two-toned grey, the firm determination of jaw to a mouth that had, she remembered with a sense of shock, held a softly sensuous quality when it touched her cheek at their meeting.

His fair lashes were long and gold-tipped, his blond hair thick but disciplined into short-styled neatness. Martha was right, she mused, feeling more surprised at the housekeeper's prescience than the turn her own thoughts had taken—the woman who took him to her bed would never lack for physical warmth.

Confusion sent a rosy flush over her cheeks when, as if

sensing the trend of her thoughts, he looked round and held her gaze for a long breathless moment. She had the oddest feeling, as brown eyes met greenish blue, that he was aware of her musings and found them impertinent. As he turned nonchalantly back to her father, Regan drew in a sharp breath of anger.

Who did he think he was, this stranger from another world? A world she didn't know and didn't care to know, if all she had heard and read about it was true. Desert and flies and hundreds of miles between homesteads. What was there about that to give him that air of confident all-knowingness? Her father's enthusiastic voice broke into her reverie.

'. . . but then, of course, to really see the results of this breeding, you'd have to go down to our summer pastures south-west of here. We have a smaller ranch down there with a few men to take care of things. Pity you didn't come a month earlier before the stock was moved.'

Bartram smiled wryly. 'A month ago I was mustering my own stock! But if you've no objection, I'd like to take a sidetrip to your summer range. I'd see a little more of the country that way.'

Phil chuckled. 'You'll do that all right! The only way to do it is by horse, unless you take the long way round by road, and even then you'd need a horse at the other end.'

'Well, that's what I'm used to. We use motor-bikes on the flat, but they're useless in hill country.' He looked round at the quietly listening women. 'Maybe now would be a good time to unload those packages I mentioned. The airline people are going to be very pleased when I go back underweight!'

Hester stirred. 'It's so sweet of her to have bothered. You must let me know what Edna needs most, Bartram, and we'll send a few things back with you.'

For a moment he looked blankly at her, then gave a slow smile. 'That would be very kind, and I'm sure she'd appreciate it.'

'If you bring in your baggage, Regan will show you to your room,' Hester said, rising and drawing Regan to her feet with a meaningful look.

A few minutes later their visitor crossed the hall to where Regan waited at the foot of the curving staircase. There was a good-sized dark brown hide suitcase in each hand, and a smaller matching one tucked securely under one long arm. She made no offer of help, sensing it would be spurned, and silently led the way to the upper floor.

Two passages branched off from the central spacious hall, and there was an air of quiet suffering about Regan's shoulders as she took the one to the left. Despite her protests, her mother had insisted on putting their visitor in the room next to hers, connected by a bathroom to each other. It would save steps for the household help, Hester had explained firmly, as Regan and their visitor would be the only occupants of the upper floor until Russ came home. Since her father's illness, one of the downstairs rooms had been made into a bedroom for her parents, thus saving Phil the exertion of stairs.

The room she led Bartram into was of a similar size to her own and having the same view through wide windows of the lake and pine-dotted hills at either side of it. In place of the prettily frilled single bed in her room, however, this one held a queen-sized double. Just as well, Regan thought now, glancing at the visitor's size and barely repressing a hysterical giggle at the thought of the Bartram she had envisaged lost in the wide expanse of bed.

'Something's funny?' the real one asked, straightening from dropping his cases on the floor near the bed, formidable suddenly in his difference from the Bartram she had imagined.

'Only you,' she returned coolly in defence against the inexplicable heightening of her pulses.

'You find me funny?' There was more of puzzlement than hurt pride in the question.

'Not you. Just that I'd—imagined you differently.'

'How differently?'

Regan shrugged and moved to the window, blinking when the descending sun's rays struck her eyes. 'Short, myopic, hornrimmed glasses . . .'

There was a short astounded silence before he spoke from just behind her right shoulder. 'Why on earth would your imagination come up with a picture like that?'

Regan was by no means a small girl, but even so she had to raise her eyes considerably to look into his face. And then her breath caught in her throat. The sun that streamed through the window made an almost white halo of his hair and fired the tips of his lashes to burnished gold. His eyes, under narrowed lids, held the green laziness of a cat's.

'Your—your name,' she whispered drily.

'My name? What's that to do with anything?'

Recovering herself, Regan stepped away from him, 'Bartram,' she mocked. 'Weren't you ever teased about that when you were young?'

'Not that I recall,' he drawled, following her across the room. 'No one's ever called me by my full name, except my mother and that only when she writes to yours. My friends call me Bart—you can too if you like.'

Meaning that she wasn't—and judging from the jut of his jaw never would be—a friend of his!

'It doesn't matter one way or the other to me,' she shrugged lightly, and moved towards the bathroom door. The lazy drawl stopped her before she reached it.

'If it makes you feel any better, I was just as wrong in my imaginings about you.'

'About me?' she asked, startled.

'Yes. You see, I'd imagined you'de be sweet, kind, dainty and very pretty—the way my mother remembers yours being years back.'

Hating her inability to stem it, Regan felt a blush rise from the base of her throat to the roots of her hair. 'Obviously you've made up your mind I'm none of those things,' she snapped.

His eyes went consideringly over the light brown luxury of waving hair to her shoulders, then examined her face with insulting slowness.

'You're pretty,' he acknowledged at last, then took away any conceit she might have had about that by adding caustically: 'But pretty is what pretty does.'

'How do you know what I do?' she demanded furiously, tilting up her chin and angling her jaw almost as tautly as his.

'I know what you nearly did this afternoon!' he bit off sharply.

'Oh, for heaven's sake,' she turned partly away from him, 'the old lady's perfectly safe, isn't she?'

'No thanks to you! I suppose it wouldn't occur to you that somewhere that old lady has relatives, friends, who care very much that she could have been badly injured or worse by a foolish girl who was busy making love with her boy-friend while she was in charge of a vehicle!'

'I was not—making love!'

'Well, I don't know what you call it here, but in Australia when we see a man and a girl with their lips glued together we call it making love.'

Stung, she threw back: 'If many of them are as inhuman as you, I'm surprised they recognise the signs! No wonder you're the age you are without being married.'

No sooner had the words left her lips than she was jerked unceremoniously against his solid front and held there firmly with one big hand at the small of her back while the other raked painfully through her hair and raised her shocked face to the white-hot anger in his.

'Wh-what are you doing?'

'What do you think I'm doing?' he returned with a blast of warm breath on her upraised face. 'Wasn't it your idea to put me on my mettle to prove I'm as human as the next man?'

'No! No, don't . . .'

A moment later she realised that she should have saved

her breath against the onslaught of his mouth covering hers with such savage pressure that air was cut off from her lungs. The lips she had imagined as being softly sensual were no such thing . . . he used them like a battering ram to force hers apart and linger there.

Dizzily, her eyes closed and she sagged against the tense thrust of his thighs, her arms circling and holding to him, her palms flat against the stinging warmth of his back muscles. A low moan, like an animal in newly realised pain, broke from her when at last he lifted his head. The hand that had tugged at her hair now cupped her ear and cheek, pressing her head back into the deep hollow of his shoulder.

He kissed her again, but this time with gentleness and all the soft sensuality she had expected his lips to hold. It was as if he deliberately sought the calm after a storm, and she relaxed against the leanly padded shoulder. She was no stranger to the feel of a man's arms round her, the scent of male skin in her nostrils, the frank arousal of his body.

Her response was simple and natural. She clung unashamedly to him, pressing the long slenderness of hip and thigh and breast to the masculine hardness of his, her mouth seeking a return to the tumultuous passion of a few moments ago. Her senses were not so numbed as to prevent her knowing that no man had ever kissed her in just that way before, sure of himself, brushing aside any objection she might have. What woman could resist such practised mastery over her senses and feelings as Regan was experiencing now?

'Oh . . .' The soft ejaculation was torn from her when he pushed her suddenly away from him, his hands like steel bands at the top of her arms. At the second when her lids fluttered open, Regan thought she could see the fleeting remnants of shocked regret in the darkened green of his eyes, and knew she was mistaken when his voice came seconds later with gravelly harshness.

'Satisfied?'

'No,' she said boldly, challenging him with emotionally sparked eyes.

A tremor of what might have been amusement quirked the outer corner of his lips as his hands dropped away from her. One of them came back up to smooth the hair she had not been aware of ruffling.

'Too bad,' he said laconically, the tension almost visibly receding from his body. 'That's all there is for the moment.' He nodded to the door behind her. 'You were about to show me what's in there?'

'It's just a bathroom.'

Brushing past her, he went to the door and opened it, glancing approvingly round its well appointed spaciousness.

'Very nice,' he commented, then noticed the door at the far side. 'Where does that lead to?'

'To—another room.'

'Yours?'

A gleam of amusement lit his eyes as they flicked over her. 'That could be an interesting arrangement—under the right circumstances.'

'Don't get excited about it,' Regan squashed. 'I'm not likely to yell for you to scrub my back in the tub!'

'Is that what your boy-friend did for you?'

'Leo's room was at the other side of the house,' she said stiffly.

He closed the bathroom door and leaned against it, regarding her through narrowed lids as he folded brawny arms across his chest.

'Your parents don't approve of him, do they?' His eyes filled with contempt. 'Not that I blame them for not taking to a man who wants all the pleasures of marriage to their daughter without the responsibility.'

Regan's eyes sparked fire. Had she really, actually, wanted this detestable creature to go on kissing her just minutes ago?

'It's not your business whether my parents approve or not,' she snapped. 'Anyway, in two months I'll be twenty-one and won't need anybody's approval of my movements.'

'Parents don't switch off caring about their offspring when the calendar reaches a certain day,' she said quietly.

'Why are you so sure of that?' she mocked. 'Are you a parent?'

'Not to my knowledge,' he conceded without a blink, 'but I do have a much younger sister who's been my responsibility since she was sixteen.'

'She has all my sympathy!'

Turning on her heel, Regan stalked out of the room and the short way along the passage to her own. After checking that the connecting bathroom door was securely locked, she threw off the clothes she had been wearing and donned thick brown corded jeans and warm gold sweatshirt before stomping along the corridor and jumping down the stairs two at a time.

'Why, Regan,' her startled mother said as she crossed the lower hall, 'you're surely not going riding now, are you? Bartram will be bringing down his little gifts from his mother, and I don't want him to be offended if you——'

'He won't be offended, Mom,' Regan threw back over her shoulder, pausing at the front door to turn her head. 'And if he considers you a friend of his, he'll let you call him Bart!'

Hester's astonished expression barely had time to register on her daughter's agitated mind before she banged out of the house, across the porch and front lawn in a direct line to the stables.

Ten minutes later her hair was streaming like a banner behind her as she prodded her own horse, Ladybird, into a gallop round the lake.

CHAPTER THREE

REGAN stayed on top of the hill only long enough to let the breeze blow a measure of cool solace over her heated brow. Thoughts too tumultuous for easy bearing down below were gradually eased into a sense of order, the kind of order she liked in her life.

The day had been fraught with emotional overtones. First Leo's half sulky insistence on a definite commitment—and that was ironic on his part, considering that the commitment would all be on her side! Then the near-accident to the woman at the crosswalk, who had been saved by a coldly furious green-eyed Australian.

Why did it have to be him of all people? Regan frowned and lifted an arm to push away the strands of light brown hair fanning against her cheek. She had been wrong about him, there were no two ways about that. Bart Kingman was a completely different proposition from the Bartram she had expected. Her head turned thoughtfully towards the house, and she half imagined a glint of white at the window of his room. At this distance it was hard to be sure.

The light wind that ruffled her hair came as an antidote to the deep blush that swept over her throat and cheeks as she remembered that kiss in his bedroom. What had possessed her to let him do it, to respond to the biting fury of his lips? She had enjoyed the kisses of boys over the years, and Leo's lovemaking to a certain point, but this kiss had nothing boyish about it. It was the kiss of a well seasoned man, a man confident and sure of himself with women, a man with the ability to draw from her with startling suddenness responses she had only vaguely guessed at possessing.

And now, she thought irritably, because she had been so

asinine as to show him the effect he had on her, he would presume he had the right to kiss her at any time he pleased! Keeping his hand in, she told herself sourly as she wheeled Ladybird around for their descent, for all the heartbroken females he had left in Australia.

But it wasn't that way at all, she discovered when she got back to the house, safely encased in the cool sheath of indifference she had decided to employ in his direction. He was again in the living room with her parents, and she noted that he had evidently showered in her absence and was now wearing a white turtle-necked sweater under dark blazer. So he *had* been watching her from the window!

Grudgingly she admitted, as she stood in the doorway, that the dark jacket emphasised the fair thickness of his hair, the bronze of his skin, but he needn't have bothered, she jeered inwardly, if his idea had been to impress her.

'Oh, there you are, Regan,' her mother said, catching sight of her and indicating a pile of wrapped packages on the round coffee table before the sofa. 'Look at all these gifts Bartra——' a smile that was almost coy in his direction—'*Bart* has brought. I could hardly wait to open mine until you got back.'

'Go ahead, Mom,' Regan said indifferently. 'I'm going up to change for dinner anyway.'

Her mother gasped, her father looked sharply at her from under beetling eyebrows, but Bart Kingman seemed completely unconcerned.

'There you are, Aunt Hester,' he drawled, 'you have permission right from the horse's mouth.'

Now it was Regan's turn to gasp at the cool insolence in his tone, but even as she turned to wheel away she caught her father's expression of astonishment mingled with—yes, *respect*—as he looked up at the younger man.

Furious, she bolted up the stairs and stormed along the passage to her room, smarting more at her father's perfidy than Bart's rudeness. Why had he capitulated so quickly to the Australian's dubious charm when none of the men she had brought home, particularly Leo, had met with much approval? Her hands ceased their movement of stripping off her clothes, and thoughtfully she reached into the double closet along one wall for her robe, a nylon swathe of Texas rose yellow.

Leo had often remarked scathingly that her father wouldn't take kindly to the Angel Gabriel himself if his intention was to carry his daughter off to a life that didn't include him. Was that why he had taken so readily to Bart, who had made it clear that as a woman Phil Taylor's daughter didn't appeal to him? Oddly, that thought held no appeal for her either.

Neither did the bathroom door, locked implacably from Bart's side of the combination.

'What arrogance!' she muttered under her breath when the door refused to yield under her pressure. 'Does he think I want to sneak around in his room while he's out?' Nothing had been further from her mind, she fumed, turning away and switching on the extractor fan against the still steamy atmosphere from Bart's shower, irked even by that evidence of his presence.

But the soothing yet stimulating spray of the massage type shower eased away the blackest of her thoughts, and by the time she had dressed in a simple but well-cut sheath dress in coffee-coloured linen she had regained most of her composure. Applying the light make-up she used with deft strokes, she reflected that it would be a simple matter to solve the problem of enforced togetherness with Bart Kingman—the Vancouver apartment was always available to any member of the family, and Russ would no doubt welcome some company.

Amber-coloured eyes looked at her stonily from the mirror. Running away to Vancouver would be like giving in, acknowledging Bart Kingman's ability to get under her skin. This was her home, her right to be here greater than his, so why should she be the one to leave it?

After slipping her nylon-clad feet into beige-heeled sandals, Regan went downstairs. A peek into the living room told her that the room was empty, save for a long figure stretched out in one of the deep armchairs close to the windows. About to turn away, she took a closer look and saw that the fair head was comfortably settled into the curve of black leather, the gold-tipped lashes tiny spear-points of light against his tanned skin. He was asleep!

Regan edged closer, her expression watchful, curious. Somehow the regular rise and fall of that wide chest irritated her, the peaceful and boyish relaxation of his face muscles an affront to her sensitivity. The mouth that had kissed hers so savagely was now no more than a firmly held masculine bow, oddly vulnerable and innocent-looking.

As innocent as a bunch of rattlesnakes, she mocked grimly and silently. Bart Kingman hadn't been innocent in that particular way for a long, long time.

Her eyes speculatively fixed on those lips, she was not aware for a second or two that the green eyes had opened suddenly, swiftly, immediately knowing.

'Seen enough?' he asked with barely veiled sarcasm.

'More than.' Regan straightened away from him, annoyed at the telltale blush on her cheeks. 'I was just wondering how long you'll be staying here.'

'Did you expect to find that information printed on my forehead?' With a lazy unwinding of his leanly packed body, he got to his feet and ran a smoothing hand over the light gleam of his hair. 'But you weren't actually examining my forehead, were you?'

The words came with mocking knowingness, and Regan's head snapped back to look scathingly at him.

'Don't flatter yourself, *Bartram*! Not one part of your anatomy interests me in any way.'

'No? That's a pity, because'—the green eyes went appreciatively over her racehorse lean form—'I find your anatomy very interesting.'

The words were right, but the wicked gleam of amusement as his eyes met hers again was not.

'And don't try to flatter me either!' she snapped. 'That might work on your females back home, but it cuts no ice with me.'

'I've heard Canada referred to as the frozen North,' he mused, narrowing his eyes to survey her more critically, 'but I wouldn't have thought that applied to you.' He breathed a heavy sigh. 'You and I seem to have got off on the wrong foot, Regan. What do you say to calling a truce?'

'A truce?' she asked, eyeing him suspiciously.

'A truce. Let's forget everything that's happened between us so far, and start afresh. However much the thought depresses you, I'm going to be here for some time and I don't think it's fair to your parents if we're at each other's throats all the time. They've been good enough to tell me to stay as long as I want to, and I wouldn't want them to regret that.'

'Oh, they won't!' said Regan, bitterness tinging her voice. 'You seem to have charmed them pretty well already—but it won't work on me,' she warned.

For once the green eyes were totally serious. 'I can assure you that I've no wish to charm you into anything more than a reasonably friendly attitude.' He held out one bronzed hand. 'Pax?'

'All right,' she said, the uncertainty in her voice driving deep inside her in a disconcerting way when the strong fingers curled round hers.

She should have been pleased that the weeks ahead would hold none of the sparks they had bounced off one another so far, but somehow she only had a sensation of letdown, as if an unusual quality of excitement had gone from her life.

True to his word, Bart maintained a politely friendly attitude towards her, a courtesy she was forced to reciprocate at least in part. As days, and then weeks, slipped by, he gave no sign of remembrance of that intimate kiss they had shared in his room on his first day at the ranch, no indication that he recalled wanting to punish her for calling his Australian manhood into question.

But Regan remembered, and mocked herself for being an idiot when her eyes were drawn to his face across the dining room table, noting the deep creases at either side of his firm mouth, the fan of lines at the outer edges of his eyes, lines burned there by a relentless Australian sun.

He spoke little about his home, except to answer Hester's queries about his mother and the rest of his family. And, sensing his reluctance to speak about a property far less prosperous than the one surrounding him now, none of the Taylors pressed him for more detail.

To Regan's surprise, Bart was accepted by the ranch employees as a substitute boss for Phil, and gradually the reins of management slid easily into place in his capable hands. His beige-coloured work clothes, and wide-brimmed hat borrowed from Phil, were very quickly a familiar sight around the ranch. He knew about horses, the breaking and training and use of them, and even Regan could pick out his tall figure, high in the saddle, in the midst of a dust-swirling confusion of men and beasts.

The only time he had reminded her of their peace pact was the night after his arrival when they were alone in the living room, Hester and Phil having retired early to bed. The phone call at ten o'clock had been from Leo, a furious Leo who demanded to know why she had changed her mind about joining him in Central America.

'I've never told you definitely that I would come,' she told him sharply, mindful of the open archway into the living room from the hall where the phone was situated.

'You weren't this sure yesterday when I left,' he had blasted angrily. 'What's wrong, have your folks been talking to you?'

'Not them, no.'

'Who, then?' Sudden suspicion had edged his voice. 'Don't tell me the little man from down under's been exerting his influence!'

'He's not like that,' she said coldly, 'and he doesn't have that kind of influence.'

The rest of the conversation was abortively useless, and when at last Regan put down the phone and walked slowly back into the living room, her knees shook with an unaccustomed tremor. Her face must have reflected her feelings, because Bart's voice was unexpectedly gentle.

'You're doing the right thing, Regan,' he had said, making no attempt to disguise the fact that he had listened to every word of the conversation. 'That kind of relationship isn't the one for a girl like you, a girl with your background . . .'

'What do you know about me or my background?' she had cried, lashing out at him because her feelings about Leo were so mixed. For months now she had thought herself in love with Leo's dark good looks, his sense of lighthearted fun making nothing of life's more serious moments. Bart Kingman's level green eyes and white-blond hair were too much of, and too sudden, a contrast for her to see him clearly as a person apart. 'I—I *cared* for Leo, and he—he loves me.'

Then, as if she and not Vicky were his young sister, he had said bluntly: 'But not enough to make you his wife. Believe me, Regan,' he got up and came to put a—yes, *brotherly*—arm around her, 'a man who really loves a woman doesn't want a hole-and-corner affair. He won't rest until he's put his ring on her finger for all the world to see that she's his woman.'

Regan, despising the gulping sob that was wrenched from her, had twisted away from that hard yet comforting arm. 'You're as old-fashioned as Mom and Dad—worse! They've never put it into words like that. Anyway,' she sniffed, looking back over her shoulder at him, 'what would you know about it? You haven't exactly leapt to put your ring on your lady love's finger!'

She turned away again and felt the stillness in him. Then, when he spoke, an odd shiver ran over her.

'I haven't reached the age I am without getting enough

knowledge to recognise the real from the worthless.' The tautness in his voice had lessened then. 'Hey, I thought we were friends now.'

And, feeling the quick sting of tears in her eyes, Regan had turned to him and been folded in those hard encompassing arms, her head against a satisfying wide shoulder. Later, she had told herself, she would feel supremely foolish at the memory of purging her sense of loss against the warm wool of his light green sweater. But it hadn't been that way at all. Whether or not his embrace was as sexless as a brother's, there was nothing sisterly about the way her body responded to the electric vibrations coming from his.

That nothing like that had entered his mind was more than obvious in the ensuing weeks when, Regan told herself in irritable pique, she might have been as cool and inanimate as the necklace he had brought for her. Although, she corrected, that wasn't a good comparison. The stone of banded agate suspended from a fine gold chain had been found on Bart's property and sent by him for professional polishing and setting. It was strangely beautiful, seeming to hold the harsh splendour of the country it came from. Pale yellow shaded to gold for the sun, and light amber merged into reddish brown for the earth. There was nothing cool or inanimate about it.

The stone looked valuable, but when Regan voiced her surprise that Bart hadn't taken advantage of such potential wealth on his property he had shaken his head with a wry smile.

'No, Regan. Scrabbling about in the dirt looking for the biggest and best gem holds no appeal for me at all.' His smile widened. 'We had our share of gold rushes in Australia too, you know, and I never could understand why a man would leave his family, most often to fend for themselves, while he went chasing rainbows.' He touched the stone held between her fingers. 'Men have died searching for that kind of wealth, but it's not the life for me. I'd never want the welfare of myself or my family to depend on luck.

I prefer the more certain way of making a living—though admittedly there's a lot of luck needed for the successful raising of stock. Drought is something we've had to live with, but at least we have food enough so that no one goes hungry.'

Regan had shivered. It was the longest speech he had made so far, and the picture he conjured up was far from attractive. What was there about that arid interior landscape that made Bart Kingman and others like him struggle against almost insurmountable odds?

Russ came home at last, bringing his usual air of exuberance with him. Watching from further back in the hall while her brother hugged each of their parents in turn, Regan reflected that instead of Russell his name should have been Russet. That was the colour of his thick, always somewhat untidy hair. The facial skin covering his good-looking features had the warm glow of health, too, and matched the sparkling brown of his eyes, which were a darker shade than Regan's.

Those eyes looked over her shoulder after he had given Regan his casually friendly brother's kiss and quick hug, lighting up as he held out a hand to their Australian visitor.

'You must be Bart . . . how are you? I've been hearing a lot of good things about your help around the place.'

Typically for Russ, there was no suggestion in his manner that he resented the way this virtual stranger had usurped his own place as their father's right hand over the weeks since he arrived. Her silent question as to how Bart would feel about relinquishing that place was answered almost immediately.

'I've been glad to fill in a bit until you got back, Russ,' he drawled, his light eyes going over Russ in swift appraisal and seeming to like what they saw. 'But now you're here, I should get down to the business I came here to do before I shove off again.' He smiled gently in Phil's direction. 'Not that I haven't enjoyed every minute of it so far, but I can't stay away from my own station for too long.'

There was a general chorus of dismay as they settled themselves in the living room. General, that was, apart from Regan. She didn't know if it was dismay or gladness that brought an extra little beat to her pulse. The time of Bart's visit had seemed to stretch indefinitely into the summer, and she had given little thought to the inevitable day of his departure. Forced now to think about it, she felt the same sense of letdown as when he had suggested the truce between them.

Her eyes flickered over to where Bart perched on the broad raised hearth, tactfully slightly apart from the family group yet one with them. The delicate stemmed crystal of the celebratory sherry glass was lost in the depths of one bronzed hand, his eyes bent to stare down at the liquid although his attitude was one of listening to the conversation going on around him.

Regan's gaze lingered on the open neck of his pale green shirt where the smooth-skinned bronze of his chest was clearly visible, moving to the powerfully muscled thighs in dark green slacks, an elbow supported on each knee.

Unaccountably, her breath seemed caught in a useless struggle with itself in her chest, the choking sensation intensifying when Bart, as if sensing her scrutiny, lifted his eyes to meet the startled amber of hers. His expression tightened as their eyes locked and held, the greenish blue of his serious and conveying—what? Warning? Regret? Regan's breath was expelled in a long audible sigh when Bart at last switched his gaze to where Russ and Phil were conversing.

How well she knew that look! It was one that said: 'Thanks for the interest, but—no, thanks!' And why shouldn't she be aware of its meaning? She had used it often enough herself on would-be admirers not to recognise the implications. Temper crackled like lightning along her nerve passages. How dared Bart Kingman imply that she had shown that kind of interest in him? Still fuming, she turned her attention on Russ when he addressed her.

'Say, Regan, I met a friend of yours the other day—somebody who I hope is now just another discarded body in your amorous past!'

'Oh?' she enquired coolly. 'Which body would that be—particularly?' Let Bart Kingman bite that off and chew it!

'Leo whatsisname.'

'Shepherd?' Regan asked, astonished. 'But you couldn't have—he left for Central America weeks ago!'

Her brother shook his head. 'No, he didn't. He told me he'd been offered another job that suited him better, but I heard from one of our fellows who knows him that he was given the chop by the research team. They found out he was trying to smuggle a chick down there with him—somebody to keep his tropical bed cosy while all the other men were expected to do without female companionship—even the married ones.'

In the pregnant hush following Russ's words, Regan stricken eyes went first to her father's greyly shocked face, then to the reluctant dawning of understanding on her mother's. Her tongue seemed to swell dryly in her mouth, blocking whatever words her brain might have thought up. Suddenly, belatedly, she knew that the good opinion of her parents mattered more—so much more—than all the Leo Shepherds and liberated ideas in the world. But she couldn't speak, find the words, to tell them that. Salvation came from an unexpected source.

'As I told you at the time, Regan,' the familiar relaxed drawl came from the fireplace, 'you were right to turn him down when he asked you to go with him.' He turned easily to divide his attention between her parents. 'I happened to be here the night she told him on the phone that she wouldn't go under circumstances like that—she hadn't realised till then all the implications. She'd been carried away with the idea of helping others less fortunate than herself, not realising what he really had in mind for her.' He looked almost tenderly at Regan. 'From the sounds of it, he'd arranged to take somebody else after you turned him down.'

'He had the nerve to ask *you* to go?' Russ turned to ask Regan, anger tautening the area round his mouth to whiteness. 'God, if I'd known that, I'd have wiped the sidewalk with him!'

'Well, there was no need for that,' said Phil, his eyes gleaming pride as they rested on Regan. 'My girl can take care of his type without any trouble at all.'

Nervously, Regan's eyes touched Bart's level look and away again. He knew how close she had come to throwing overboard the tenets of her upbringing, the trust and faith of her parents. It was painfully obvious that her mother was aware of that fact too when, asking Regan to help her lay the table for dinner, she looked severe as she shook out the beige linen cloth to cover the oval table.

'You really thought about going with Leo to Central America, didn't you, Regan?' she asked, not looking at her daughter as she smoothed the creases from the cloth.

'Yes,' Regan said simply.

'Knowing what he would expect from you?'

'Yes.'

Hester went to the china cabinet and lifted the lid of the cutlery chest, selecting the items they would need for that night's dinner.

'What changed your mind? Was it—your father?'

'Partly—well, maybe mostly,' Regan admitted honestly, picking up half of the cutlery and setting places at her half of the table. 'I couldn't bear for him to think that I—that . . .'

'It would have killed him, Regan,' said Hester calmly, seeming not to feel the dramatic import of her words as she straightened knives and forks and coffee spoons in their places. 'To him you're still the little girl you always were, loving, beautiful in looks and nature, adoring him . . .'

'I do adore him, Mom,' Regan said unsteadily. 'So much that I couldn't ever bear anything to happen to him.' The soft brown of her eyes appealed to her mother. 'He's not terribly ill, Mom, is he? I mean . . .'

'Of course he's not,' Hester Taylor returned crisply, pausing to regard her daughter with troubled eyes. 'He just has to be rested and relaxed and kept free from unnecessary worries—which means the excursion you were planning with Leo Shepherd.'

'Well, he doesn't have to worry about that any more. I'm off men in general now,' Regan said moodily, sliding salt and pepper containers to either end of the large table.

Hester chuckled unexpectedly. 'For how long? You've been saying that regularly for the past four years. Tell me, honey,' she asked casually, 'what do you think of Bart? As a man, I mean. I know from reading between the lines of Edna's letters that she's concerned that he hasn't yet married, and he seems a tremendously attractive man to me.'

'Bart?' Regan thought for a moment before going on slowly. 'Yes, he's very attractive—in a physical kind of way. He has all the outer assets of a woman's dream man, but . . .'

'But?'

'Well, I don't know. He's so—self-contained somehow,' Regan attempted to explain, '—as if he doesn't need anyone at all, let alone a mere woman.'

'Yet he's very understanding, kind, generous—why, look at the necklace he brought for you, dear,' Hester puzzled. 'For a man who has a struggle to barely survive, that was a more than generous gesture.'

'Well, of course he's not going to let his more prosperous relatives think he can't afford a reasonable gift!' Regan expostulated, moving to the door. 'That necklace is probably something he intended for his wife-to-be once upon a time.'

'Mmm . . . yes,' her mother returned absently.

Upstairs, Regan quickly stripped off her close-fitting jeans and loose top, reaching for her robe and tying it round her before going to the bathroom for her shower.

The door yielded at once to her pressure, and she stared

aghast at the bronzed male figure newly emerged from the shower. A magnificent figure, part of her mind admitted, while the other three quarters of it reacted with violent prudishness to the virile maleness of it. Unperturbed, Bart reached for a bath towel and draped it round his hips.

'Oh ...' said Regan with inadequate voice power. 'I—I'm sorry, I didn't know ...' Her voice trailed off, then, with gathering indignation, she said aggressively: 'Why don't you lock the door when you're using the bath?'

Mocking, sarcastic, his voice came back at her. 'I wouldn't have thought a girl of your wide experience could be set off course by the sight of a man in his shower.'

'Certainly not,' said Regan with commendable dignity, which she hoped would cover the untruth of what she said. Retreating, she turned back with one hand on the door. 'I—I should thank you ... for what you did down there.'

'No, you shouldn't,' he returned briefly, reaching with one hand for his black electric shaver box and flipping it open with the other. 'I did it for your parents' sake, not yours.'

Nonplussed, she stared at the naked brown of his back.

'You see, Regan,' he turned to face her, his jaw held in an uncompromising line, 'I happen to think you're the most spoiled, selfish, self-dominated person in the world. Your people are dinkum, but you're something else again.'

'What gives you the right to judge, Bart Kingman?' she flared, blinking against the weak tears threatening to fill her eyes. 'You don't know anything about me, but you go around acting as if—as if you're God or something! For your information, and not because it's any of your business, I didn't go with Leo because I couldn't hurt my parents that way. Is that selfish?'

'Couldn't hurt your parents!' he said disgustedly, then took a long stride forward and gripped her wrist hurtfully. 'You didn't go with him because you were afraid! Afraid of facing up to the fact that what he wanted from you is what any man wants from a woman. A little sweetness, a little tenderness—and a lot of loving. All three of which qualities you're sadly lacking in—particularly the last!'

The filmy material of Regan's robe tautened over the rounded curves of her breasts as she inhaled with angry deepness. Sherry eyes sparked off the glacial gleam of light green as she glared with impotent rage at her male tormentor.

'What makes you such a damned expert?' she demanded explosively. 'Do women materialise out of the sand in that God-forsaken country you call home?'

That got him, she told herself triumphantly, seeing the quick hardening of his jaw as he clenched his teeth together. A second later she felt a quiver of apprehension run over her spine when his hand tightened on her wrist and threatened to snap the fine bones there. He would do that, she marvelled, looking up at the impassive harshness bitten deep into his features. It seemed anticlimactic when he suddenly threw her arm from him and stepped away from her.

'Go away, Regan,' he said heavily, 'before I do something I might regret for your family's sake.'

His back was again presented to Regan as he lifted his shaver from its case and plugged it in at the outlet, his eyes in the mirror intent only on the contours of his chin and mouth area as he ran the blades across his skin.

'Is this your idea of a truce?' Regan demanded of his mirrored image.

'Consider the truce cancelled.' His eyes met hers briefly in reflection, then returned to the grooming process.

'That suits me,' Regan flung at him, and flounced out, locking the door behind her as noisily as possible although she knew that the razor's hum would deaden it somewhat.

Pacing to the window of her prettily appointed room, she reflected furiously that the sooner Bart Kingman went back to Australia the happier she would be. How dared he presume to judge her character and find it wanting?

Later, after her shower, she looked thoughtfully at the faint blue-black of bruises forming on her wrist and her mouth compressed to a tight line. What would her parents think of their precious Bart if they could see the livid marks of his temper?

For reasons unknown, even to herself, Regan chose a dress with wide billowing sleeves caught just below the wrists in a bell effect.

CHAPTER FOUR

'WELL, I think he's dreamy, whatever you say.'

Patty stretched luxuriously on the lounger beside Regan's, squinting against the sun that glinted off the lake a bare few yards away from where the two girls were relaxing. They had been in for a swim, but agreed with goosepimpled arms that the water could bear a little warming up from the sun.

Regan donned sunglasses that covered half her face and looked at her friend. 'It's all very fine for you to say that,' she said waspishly. 'You don't have to live in the same house with him.'

Patty smiled, her eyes closed, fair skin already tinged pink from the sun. The blue floral material of her one-piece suit seemed to emphasise the softly feminine curves of her figure, in contrast to Regan's bikini which delineated only briefly her salient points and left a great deal of firm-fleshed skin showing.

'I can think of a dozen or more females who'd give anything they have, including their virtue, to spend a few nights under the same roof as Bart Kingman,' Patty murmured lazily.

'Only because they don't know what he's really like!' Regan retorted, sinking back into the padded comfort of her lounger before twisting her head back to look at Patty. 'Anyway, I didn't realise he knew that many females in Rivertown.'

'I didn't say he knew them,' Patty chuckled. 'Just that they'd like to know him a whole lot better.'

'They wouldn't if they knew him,' Regan repeated, subsiding again into cushioned comfort. 'I've never known anybody so—so full of himself, so sure that he's right all the time . . .'

'You know what, Regan?' Patty rolled over to her stomach and looked amusedly over at her lithely stretched out friend. 'I think you're mad because he isn't what you'd expected him to be. He's a long way from the Humphrey Davidson type!'

'At least Humphrey didn't throw his weight around and think he was God's answer to women!'

'He wasn't equipped to do that,' Patty returned drily. 'But Bart's another proposition altogether.' She looked curiously at her friend. 'I'd have said he was just the type you'd go for—or at least the type of man you need. Somebody who wouldn't let you get your own way too much.'

'Huh! The man who can master me hasn't been born yet!'

'That could be construed as a challenge,' came a familiar drawl, and both girls jerked their heads in the direction of the voice, seeing two male figures dressed in nothing but swimming briefs.

Russ, his body of the same long leanness as Regan's except that he was taller, wore dark red, while Bart's briefs were a startling white against the bronze of his skin.

While Regan glared wordlessly at Bart, ignoring the swell of tanned chest above neatly tapered hips—hadn't she seen him in all his natural glory in the bathroom they shared?—Russ came between the two loungers and tipped Patty's up to one side so that she fell spluttering in the sand.

Grinning, he bent and hoisted the quiescent Patty into his arms and made for the water, saying to Bart over his shoulder: 'Come on Bart, get Regan on her feet.'

Bart made no attempt to set Regan on her feet once he had bent and picked her up lithely from the lounger, ignoring her indignant hiss to put her down that instant. The feel of his hard arms on her waist and legs, the warmth of his lower chest against her midriff, added fuel to her incensed cries as he waded stoically into the frigid water.

'Put me *down*!' she gritted through white clenched teeth, and gasped when he did just that, dropping her vertically into the dark greenish-blue water.

It was deeper than she had expected. Her head was the last to submerge, and she felt the cold rush of water into her mouth, her nose, her ears, and came up groping wildly for the security of Bart's wide shoulders. Finding herself grabbing at empty air, she panicked and went under a second time, all her deeply ingrained water skills fleeing from her.

Then she felt the long muscled arms reach down to pluck her from the water as easily as if she were a child, and her arms clung desperately to him as he strode back to the strip of sand. Against her ear was the reassuringly steady beat of his heart—and something else. The uncontrollable shaking of his chest had nothing to do with the lake's coldness . . . he was laughing at her!

'Put me down!' she gasped when he halted at the lounger and continued to hold her.

'You're sure you want me to?' The green eyes laughed unabashedly into hers. 'It wasn't too successful the last time I put you down when you ordered it.'

'I could have—d-drowned!' she chattered, unwinding the arm she had battened round his neck and pushing unavailingly against his chest.

'I'm sorry,' he grinned unrepentantly. 'I thought you could swim.'

'Of c-course I can swim! I've been s-swimming since I was th-three.' Regan twisted against him again. 'Put me down!'

'Didn't your mother ever teach you the magic word?' he questioned maddeningly.

'Please!' she gritted, and found herself dumped unceremoniously on the lounger, her terry robe thrown at her.

'Better save your towel for drying your hair, you look like a drowned rat.'

'Thanks!'

Before she had time to lift the towel to her head, Bart had gone. Back to the water, striding in and then diving as if it was no colder than a tepid bath. Balefully, she watched him streak to the raft where Patty and Russ sat side by side, evidently deep in conversation. Something about the closeness of their heads told her that neither of them would welcome a third party on the raft, but she was wrong. Sounds of laughter floated back to her as she rubbed vigorously at her hair, Patty's light and feminine, Russ's in a midtone, and Bart's deepest of all.

Was he telling them about her near-drowning, sharing his own amusement at her spluttering attempts to grab him? Hurt streaked through her, and suddenly she felt left out, unwanted by the three who seemed to be enjoying themselves hugely. It was a new feeling for her, and she contemplated it as she drew her comb through the tangled mass of her hair, wincing irritably when it dragged at the roots.

Being ignored by a fun-bent group was something that had never happened to Regan before—always it was she at the centre of activity. So it must be something to do with Bart Kingman.

Bart, who made no bones about his dislike of her in private, but who subtly displayed a brotherly air of tolerance in public.

So lost in thought was she that she failed to hear Russ's approach until he was splashing towards her from the shallows, smiling his concern as he drew near Regan. At least one of them cared about her, she thought sourly, laying down her comb and leaning back on the thick padding.

'Hi, Sis. I came to get the beach ball, the three of us are going to have a mini-game of water polo.'

'Jolly!' Regan remarked frigidly.

'Too bad you can't join us—Bart said you weren't feeling up to the cold water today.'

'Oh, he did, did he?'

Russ turned back to look questioningly at her. 'What's wrong, Sis? You don't seem to like Bart for some reason, and he's one of the most likeable guys I've ever known. Why do you keep brushing him up the wrong way?'

'*I*—?' Regan stared speechlessly at her brother. 'What about him? He treats me like a stick of furniture, except for the odd time he deigns to look down that long nose of his and put me in my place about something!'

Russ came back slowly to stand over her, the beach ball tucked under one lightly tanned arm. He looked at Regan speculatively for a long moment, then unexpectedly chuckled.

'I've worked out what's wrong with you,' he said with brotherly candour. 'You're mad because Bart hasn't fallen at your feet like all the other males who drift by your net!'

Regan snapped: 'Don't be ridiculous!' and snapped her sunglasses on to her nose, glaring furiously through the smoky lenses to where the cause of their dissension lay lazily on the raft, propped up on one elbow to look down at the seemingly entranced Patty.

'... the only reason I can think of,' Russ was saying. 'I like him a lot, Mom and Dad think he's great——'

'So does Patty by the looks of it,' Regan pointed out acidly, and Russ turned to look at the raft.

'Mmm,' he said thoughtfully after a few moments. 'I think I'll have to go and split up that little twosome.'

So saying, he strode away from Regan, leaving the imprint of his long feet in the damp sand at the lake's edge. She watched him swim out to the raft, and didn't know if it was her over-active imagination that made her think Bart's head jerked up with an irritable motion when Russ threw the ball from the water, landing it on Patty's midriff.

Minutes later, however, the three were in the water with the ball, Russ gentling his throws in Patty's direction. Irritably, Regan reflected that at least Bart's show of interest in Patty's company had jolted her brother into a different awareness of her lifelong friend.

She was reading a fashion magazine when the three splashed back to shore and barely glanced at them as they settled round her, Patty in the other lounger with Russ on the sand beside her chair, Bart separating himself from the group by moving a few yards off to Regan's right.

'Anybody else like a smoke?' Russ asked, reaching for the shirt he had abandoned on the sand.

Bart shook his head. 'No, thanks. I gave it up a couple of years ago.'

Mr Perfection, Regan sneered inwardly, in control of all his vices and shortcomings.

'Wish I could, though I don't indulge too much.' Jokingly, Russ offered the pack to Patty. 'How about you, Patty?'

'You know I don't smoke, Russ,' she protested gently, hurt edging her voice at his forgetfulness.

'That's good,' Bart approved. 'Smoking certainly doesn't add to a woman's attractiveness.'

'I'll have one, Russ,' Regan said abruptly.

'*You?*' Russ stared at her incredulously. 'I've never seen you smoke.'

'We haven't been together that much lately,' Regan returned drily, putting out a hand to the opened pack so that Russ automatically held it out for her. In the same dazed manner he flicked his lighter for her. 'Do the folks know you smoke?'

Regan shrugged lightly and puffed a cloud into the air. 'Oh, Dad's as old-fashioned as Bart here about women smoking. He's in the Stone Age where emancipation for women's concerned.'

'Who can blame him for that when his daughter uses her freedom to pollute her health?' came the distinctive accent.

'I know what I'm doing!' Regan snapped, drawing in a deep lungful of smoke to prove her point and promptly coughing as her lungs rejected the alien product.

'Oh, Regan, put it out,' Patty said with concerned impatience. 'Anyway, here comes your mother.'

'What?' Wildly, Regan looked round and her mother was indeed advancing along the beach, her feet picking their way unsteadily over the sand. Panicking, Regan's fingers froze round the cigarette. Independence flew from her, and she knew she couldn't face her mother's shock at seeing her only daughter indulge in the habit she deplored in her son. Then the problem was taken out of Regan's hands when a bronzed figure came to crouch beside her chair, blocking her mother's view while a swift transfer of the cigarette took place.

'Well, how did the first swim of the year go?' Hester asked indulgently as she came up to them. 'I imagine the water was—why, Bart, I didn't know you smoke!'

'I don't very much, Aunt Hester,' he returned easily, putting the cigarette to his mouth and drawing in with remembered skill. 'Only at times of severe stress.' His eyes narrowed ironically on Regan.

To her surprise, her mother chuckled. 'Then the water must have been colder even than I imagined! You'd better all come up to the house for a warm drink.' Her smile encompassed them all. 'I really came down to see how many we'd be for dinner—can you stay, Patty? We'd love to have you stay.'

'Thanks, Mrs Taylor,' Patty said regretfully, 'but I promised Dad I'd be back to cook dinner.' She looked at her watch. 'In fact, I should have left half an hour ago.'

'It seems there's no end to your accomplishments, Patty,' Bart put in softly, his eyes admiring as they rested on the fair girl. 'Your father's a lucky man.'

Patty blushed faintly and Russ looked thoughtful again as he put down a hand to help her to her feet.

'Why don't we all go dancing tonight?' Russ's question was for all of them, but his eyes rested seriously on Patty's upturned face. 'Our local Saturday night barn dance is something Bart should see before he goes back to Australia.'

If there was underlying thankfulness at the prospect of their visitor's return to his homeland, Bart at least appeared not to catch it.

'I'd like that, Russ.' He smiled engagingly at Patty. 'You'll have to teach me the steps, I'm afraid.'

'Oh, there's nothing to it really,' Patty said eagerly, falling into step with him and seeming to forget Regan and

Russ behind them. Mrs Taylor had gone on ahead.

'Give me a hand to put the chairs away, will you, Regan?' Russ said tersely, folding up the lounger Patty had used, his movements savagely jerky.

Silence was maintained between them as they cleared away the chairs, carrying them to the boathouse situated on the grassy area behind the strip of beach. Only when they were walking up to the house did Regan look up into her brother's stormy-looking face.

'You're not just going to let him waltz off with Patty, are you?' she scorned.

'That's up to Patty,' he said tightly, acknowledging for the first time in Regan's hearing that Patty meant more to him than his kid sister's friend.

'Oh, don't be such a dope! Don't you know that Patty's been crazy about you for years?'

'She has?' Russ seemed genuinely startled. 'I guess I—I've taken it for granted that she'll always be here. I never thought about somebody like Bart coming along . . .'

'And you just sit back and let him take her away!' Regan cried with impotent fury.

'No, I won't.' Russ put a hand on her arm when they reached the veranda. 'Look, Regan, you can help me. Tonight, at the dance, see that you're the one he dances with, not Patty.'

She stared at him aghast. 'How can I do that?'

'Oh, come on. You've never had any trouble getting men to dance with you.'

'Men are one thing . . . Bart Kingman's something else! Russ, he hates me. I'm the last one he'd want to dance with.'

Russ looked harassed. 'Well, wear something sexy, something to catch his interest.'

Regan marched forcefully up the steps. 'If I went in the nude, the only interest I'd stir up in him would be a lecture on how proper young ladies should appear in public!'

Nevertheless, Regan took extra care with her preparations that night. Liquid make-up flowed smoothly on to form a matt finish, leaving glowing highlights on cheeks and forehead. Light brown eye-shadow gave depth to her amber eyes, and as an afterthought she added a pencil-slim line of darker brown at the edge of her lids. Surveying the effect, she decided that her appearance was more deliberately provocative than it had ever been before. That impression was heightened when she stepped into her dress of vibrant burnt orange and outlined her lips in a matching shade.

'That should be sexy enough for you, Russ,' she muttered, eyeing the low plunging neckline supported mainly by her own firm young curves.

The two men were in the hall when Regan went down, Bart with his back to her, Russ just putting down the telephone he had been using.

'Wow, Sis!' he grinned at her, 'there'll be a few more hearts strewn around your feet when the locals see you in that!'

Bart was slow to turn round, and Regan had ample time to note that, like Russ, he looked neat but casual in high-necked silk-like sweater and dark jacket. Watching his reaction to her appearance, she detected a flickering gleam of bare masculine appreciation in the eyes that went over her from top to toe. Then the eyes came back to rest pointedly on the neckline that plunged between her breasts.

'Russ, I thought you said this wasn't a dress-up affair—or should I say dress-down?' Insolently, his eyes probed the curving areas covered briefly by the material, and Regan felt as if that look dissolved the light fabric and left her naked for his inspection.

Lifting the lacy wool stole she held over her arm, Regan deliberately draped it across her shoulders and pulled it tight across her as she led the way into the living room to say goodnight to her parents.

'You look even more beautiful than usual, honey,' her father said as she bent to kiss him, adding with mock resignation: 'I suppose this means we'll be having a few more anxious young fellows beating a path to our door!'

'Don't worry about that, Dad,' Russ straightened up from bestowing a light kiss on his mother's cheek. 'Bart and I are plenty big enough to repel all comers!'

His words remained with Regan as she walked between the two tall men to the front door and down the steps. Certainly Bart was big enough to discourage Regan's unwelcome admirers, but she couldn't for the life of her ever imagine him being interested enough to do so.

Russ got out the family Buick, more comfortably spacious than either his own or Regan's sports type cars, and in another moment Regan found herself still between the two men, but closely wedged on the bench seat across the front of the car. It was strangely disturbing to feel the hard pressure of Bart's thigh against hers, to know that if she bent her head back even slightly it would rest on the arm he had stretched along the seat back behind her.

'I just phoned Patty to tell her we were on our way,' Russ said, aiming the car townwards and accelerating to the rapid speed he liked to drive at. He chuckled. 'From the way she sounded, she'd been ready for hours and we were keeping her waiting.'

'Patty's always like that,' Regan said into the darkness surrounding them. 'When we were in Europe, we were always the first to arrive when we'd arranged to meet anybody.'

'That must have been hell for you, Regan,' Russ returned drily.

'Punctuality's a good habit to cultivate,' Bart put in pontifically, and Regan sighed impatiently. Did he always have to be on the side of law and order, liking everything to unfold like a graceful minuet of old? Didn't he ever have moments of weakness, moments when he threw caution to the winds and dived into life without the security of a set pattern to guide him?

The exciting hardness of his body was warm against her

side, but had he even noticed her own softness or the lightly intoxicating perfume she had used? The scent filled her own nostrils, stirred her own senses, but she would guarantee that if Bart Kingman had noticed it at all it was only to disparage the feminine need to excite the male.

Russ slowed, then stopped the car in front of the service station. Patty materialised from the doorway of the adjoining bungalow as if she had been waiting there, and before Russ could move Bart was out of the car and holding the rear door open for her, murmuring something complimentary as he followed her in and closed the door behind them.

'Hi, Regan, Russ,' Patty said breathlessly, then turned to smile up at Bart beside her. 'You didn't have to come in the back with me, Bart. It's not far to town from here.'

'No,' he admitted, a smile in his voice, 'but it was getting a bit crowded up in front.'

Regan breathed deeply and swivelled her head to the front as Russ started the car into motion again. What had he meant by that? Crowded, indeed! She could think of umpteen men who would be delirious at the thought of being pressed intimately against her side!

The pleasant conversation going on at the rear only served to point up the chagrined silence at the front of the car. Russ's face, dimly illuminated from the dashboard, had a set look about it, and Regan felt a surge of fury engulf her. She and Russ had had the usual ups and downs between brother and sister, but she cared deeply about his happiness. A happiness which Bart Kingman now seemed bent on destroying. It didn't matter to her that Russ had only now become aware of a special feeling for Patty . . . there had always been an unspoken assumption in Regan's mind at least that sooner or later Russ and Patty would make a pair.

So Regan gritted her teeth and set out to charm their Australian visitor, disregarding all the signs which she instinctively recognised as total uninterest on his part. That she had set herself an almost impossible task was evident from the moment they entered the community hall.

Nearly all of the younger crowd of the district were packed into the wood siding building. Its walls seemed to vibrate with the sound of loud music and the movement of bodies gyrating in time to the recorded music coming from loudspeakers. Canned rhythm alternated with a four-man band for the country style dances intended to satisfy the sprinkling of a more mature element.

By a stroke of fortune, the two men secured a table at the rear of the room where a seating area had been arranged. Two elderly couples, obvious visitors to the vicinity, had given up their attempts to ignore the assault on eardrums and vacated the hall with pained expressions on their faces.

'Phew!' Bart tugged at the high neck of his sweater. 'I'm glad you suggested leaving our jackets in the car, Russ. It's pretty unbearable, isn't it? Still,' he turned to smile at Patty, who had somehow been installed beside him, 'just looking at you girls in your dresses is enough to cool a man off considerably.' His eyes went appreciatively over Patty's discreetly bared shoulders emerging from her blue patterned sundress.

Regan, knowing that the remark had been meant for Patty alone, said drily: 'A woman's intention in wearing a revealing dress isn't to *cool* a man's blood!'

The green eyes narrowed and went lazily to the deep plunge of her dress. 'Oh, I don't know. From my point of view, a woman who strives too hard to expose her charms leaves me stone cold. I like a little mystery.'

Regan drew in a sharp outraged breath, while Patty frowned and gave Bart a thoughtful sideways look. Russ, sensing an explosion from his volatile sister, stepped quickly into the breach.

'How about a drink? What would you like, girls?'

Patty decided on plain ginger ale, and Regan said shortly

that she'd have the same with an addition of rye whisky. Her eyes held a defiant glitter as they met Bart's, but he made no comment on her choice.

'I'll come and help,' he offered, rising and following Russ to the crowded corner where a bar counter had been erected.

'Regan, what's wrong with you and Bart?' Patty asked as soon as the men were out of earshot. Her blue eyes looked anxiously across the table at her friend. 'You seem to rile each other all the time.'

'It's hard to get along with somebody as opinionated as he is,' Regan bit off sharply.

'But he's not really like that,' Patty protested. 'If you'd just give him a chance, Regan, you'd find he's really nice and very interesting when he talks about Australia. I *like* him,' she ended on a softly stubborn note.

'And he likes you, that's plain to see!' Regan looked thoughtfully at the other girl. 'What about Russ?—or don't you care for him any more now that you've met Mr Superman?'

'Oh, Regan!' A flamelike blush heightened the china blue of Patty's eyes. 'A man like Bart Kingman wouldn't be interested in somebody like me.'

'No?' Regan's voice was hard. 'You're just the kind he would go for, all wide-eyed femininity, hanging on his every word.'

Patty mouth opened in an indignant gasp, but the men's return at that moment precluded her saying any more.

The music which had stopped for a brief interval, started again just after the men had resettled themselves in their chairs, tall glasses of beer before them. Bart looked enquiringly down at Patty.

'Care to try your luck at teaching an Aussie some of your Western dances?'

Patty smiled fleetingly up into his face and nodded, avoiding Regan's eyes when she stood up and moved away with Bart. A prickle of irritation crossed Regan's skin when she saw the big brown hand curl round Patty's pale-skinned arm to lead her to the floor.

'Do you have to sit there like a stick and let him take over?' she snapped waspishly to Russ, who withdrew his moody gaze from the other couple and directed it at his sister.

'What was I supposed to do? Beat my chest and yell "hands off my girl?"' Sobered suddenly by the sound of his own possessive words, Russ turned back to the dance floor and looked with surprised speculation at the animatedly laughing Patty. All at once, Regan's irritation fled and was replaced by a wave of compassion for her brother.

'I wouldn't worry,' she advised, 'he's not Patty's type.'

'I wouldn't be too sure of that,' Russ returned slowly, his eyes on the Australian's blond head that seemed to tower over the other dancers. 'Strikes me he's the kind any woman would go for. Good-looking he-man stuff.'

'Huh! Well, here's one woman you can count out of that number!'

'Can I?' Russ looked thoughtfully at his sister. 'Sure you haven't fallen for him? Could be that's what all the static between you is about.' He chuckled. 'And you'd go down with your head bloodied before you'd admit it!'

Shock jolted through Regan and left her breathless. There was no way Bart Kingman's arrogance could appeal to her. She loathed the kind of person, man or woman, who was always so sure of being right, of being the last word of judgment on any matter within his sphere. And yet . . . there was the kiss he had thrust on her on his first day at the ranch. Masterfully punishing at first, it had then turned into something entirely different. Questing, with a hint of underlying tenderness that would disarm any woman he had set his mind on possessing.

'No,' she murmured, mostly to herself, but Russ lifted one sardonic brow as he smiled knowingly into her bewildered face. 'Don't be ridiculous, Russ,' she snapped, recovering herself. 'He'd have to do more than bloody my head to get me to fall for *him*!'

'Mmm. Well, by the looks of it, you won't have to worry on that score.'

Regan's eyes followed his to where Bart, already familiar with the steps of a fairly intricate dance, swung a smiling Patty round the floor, firm hands at her femininely indented waist. A feeling totally unfamiliar in its intensity washed over Regan. Was it envy of Patty's sweet prettiness, of the obvious attraction it had for Bart?

Ridiculous, she told herself, and deliberately pulled her eyes from the dancing pair to scan the room. Her gaze rested thoughtfully on the figure of a dark-haired girl seated nearby. The vivacious Jess Hartman was the one person in the world Patty openly admitted to disliking, mainly because Russ had been enamoured of her a year or so ago. It was an affair that burnt brightly for a while, then fizzled out when Russ returned to university. The two were still on amicable terms, however.

'Russ, why don't you ask Jess to dance? She's sitting alone over there.'

Russ glanced casually over at the other girl, then took a moody gulp at his beer. 'I'm not in the mood for dancing,' he said grumpily.

'It's what you came here to do, isn't it?'

'Not with Jess.'

Regan frowned at him impatiently. There were times when she could cheerfully shake her mule-like brother, and this was one of them.

'So you're going to sit there like the wrath of God and let Patty play you off against Bart Kingman?'

Russ looked sharply at her, then to the oblivious couple on the dance floor, and finally back to Jess, who had seen them and was smiling fetchingly in their direction.

Decisively quiet, he said: 'No, I'm not,' and rose, hesitating as he looked down at his sister. 'What about you, Sis? I don't want to leave you alone here.'

Airily, she waved him away. 'Somebody'll take pity on me once my brooding brother is off the scene.'

Still Russ hesitated. 'As long as the somebody isn't Will Deighton,' he said soberly. 'I saw him at the bar a while ago. You know Dad said he'd take a horsewhip to him if he came near you again.'

'Oh, for heaven's sake, Russ, it wasn't his fault the car got stuck in a drift! Dad's so old-fashioned——'

'So am I when it comes to the Will Deightons of this world,' Russ retorted grimly. 'You're not to have anything to do with him, Regan, understand?'

'I'm not eighteen any more, Russ,' she said hotly. 'If he asks me to dance, I intend to accept!'

Russ gave her a tightlipped nod and departed to the beaming Jess. Regan looked angrily round for a glimpse of the man in question. Two years ago she had been a naïve schoolgirl flattered by the attractions of a much older man; now she was half curious about how he would affect her maturer self.

She and Will had dated several times before the fatal night when, returning from having dinner in a plush Kamloops restaurant, Will had turned off into a side road with an intent Regan didn't at first understand. Even the snowdrift that enveloped the entire underbody of the car in an icy grip seemed part of Will's smoothly laid plans, and he was unperturbed about their predicament when he turned to take her into his arms.

Even in the overheated atmosphere of the community hall now Regan shivered, remembering the panic that had swept over her when the playfully light kisses became something deeper, frightening in their intensity. She had even cried, she recalled, and it was that that cooled Will's ardour and sent him stamping bad-temperedly out into the snow to dig the car out. Despite his anger-directed efforts, it was almost four in the morning before they drove up to the ranch house.

A house still blazing with lights and irate parents whose

anxiety turned to wrath as soon as they had assured themselves that their daughter was unharmed. Will, sensing the reception he would get, paused only long enough to let Regan out of the car, then sped on his way. She hadn't seen him since.

CHAPTER FIVE

'REGAN! Is it really you?'

The familiar voice struck against her memory chords, and Regan looked up to where Will stood beside the table, expecting the old triphammer effect he had always had on her heart. Her eyes widened in surprise.

Surely a mere two years couldn't have changed Will's suavely sophisticated appearance into this slightly overblown and definitely ageing male? Yet he must only be two or three years older than Bart, she thought dazedly, picturing the Australian's tightly knit figure and comparing it unfavourably with Will's well-fed frame.

'Yes,' she said faintly, 'it's me, Will.'

'You've certainly changed, Regan, I hardly recognised you.' He sat in Bart's chair opposite without invitation and let his eyes rove over the shining waves of her light brown hair, the confident expertness of her make-up, and going at last to the sweep of bare skin visible between the scanty folds of her dress. 'You've—grown up in two years,' he smiled appreciatively, and Regan instantly wished that she had worn a different dress.

'Mm-hm,' she agreed nonchalantly, her eyes looking levelly into the brown of his, which had once struck her as being dashingly romantic but now looked an indeterminate mud colour. 'Two years can make quite a difference.'

He smiled, reminding her vaguely of the attraction he had had for her. 'I can tell you wouldn't burst into maidenly tears this time if we ran into a snowdrift!'

'Wrong time of year for drifts, Will. In fact, wrong period as far as you and I are concerned.'

He cocked one eyebrow with practised roguery. 'I could interpret that as a challenge to prove you wrong.'

Regan laughed shortly. 'If you can find a drift to get us stuck in at this time of year, Will, I'll gladly agree to go with you.'

'It might be worth arranging a snowfall at that,' he said speculatively, looking up when Patty and Bart returned to the table, Western music finished temporarily.

Patty was no longer smiling, her eyes holding a hurt and faintly withdrawn look as she painstakingly presented her back to where Russ leaned over Jess at her table, laughing at something she had said. Bart's eyes went in swift appraisal over Will as he stood up to return Bart's seat, and Regan introduced them briefly.

'Will Deighton—Bart Kingman, my cousin from Australia.'

The two men shook hands and exchanged a few pleasantries before Bart sat down and took a long draught of his beer. The look he sent across to Regan held a faintly sardonic amusement, as if he knew all the intimate details of her relationship with Will and found them laughable.

When the heavy beat of recorded music started a moment later, Russ came over and asked Patty to dance. For a second or two, the fair girl seemed about to refuse, then she got to her feet and walked stiffly with Russ to the floor.

'Care to dance, Regan?' Will asked, then glanced down at Bart. 'If you've no objection?'

Bart spread his hands dismissingly. 'None at all,' he drawled, then a smile appeared in his green eyes as he looked across at Regan. 'I'm not much fun for my—cousin. This isn't my style of dancing.'

'It's not my father's, either!' flashed Regan as she got to her feet, contempt visible in every swish of her dress as she led the way to the dance floor.

Her movements were automatic at first, conscious as she was of Bart's supercilious gaze burning her back. But then the pagan rhythm reached out to her as it always did, the music fusing with some deep-felt longing inside her, orchestrating the primitive movement of her entire body.

She forgot Bart, forgot Will's admiringly lascivious eyes, giving herself up to the mindless response of blood and heartbeat to the drowning crescendo of music flooding her mind.

This was where she was most truly herself, in touch with the eternal woman that she was, recognising and welcoming the wordless longings she knew would be satisfied one day . . . by someone special . . . the nameless, faceless man who would make her one with him . . .

She blinked rapidly once or twice, suddenly aware that the music had ceased, that Will's arm was hugging her waist and drawing her to him.

'You're beautiful, Regan,' he murmured at her ear. 'I've never seen anybody dance like you, you're a natural.'

'Don't, Will,' she pulled away, 'it's so hot in here.'

Taking that as an invitation, Will's arm tightened on her waist and before she could collect her scattered senses he had led her outside, away from the heat and noise, coming to a halt under the spreading branches of a shade tree beside the building.

'Regan,' he said huskily, his arms firm round her, pushing her back until she felt the deeply indented bark pressing against her flesh. Wasting no more time on words, Will pressed his mouth hotly to hers in a kiss that sent nausea leaping from her stomach to her throat.

What was she doing out here alone with Will Deighton? In a moment of weakness, she longed for Russ to sense her predicament and come out in search of her.

Deliverance came not from her brother, however, but from a rangy white-topped figure who drawled in an accent that was familiarly dear at that moment,

'Regan? They're playing my kind of music now, so why don't you come and dance with your poor Aussie cousin?' He neatly extracted Regan from Will's clutching hold. 'You don't mind, chum, do you?'

Not waiting for Will's reply, he spirited Regan away and they were entering the hall when she found her breath.

'Will you please stop butting in and "saving" me!' she hissed through her teeth. 'I'm perfectly capable of taking care of myself!'

'Really?' Bart drew her none too gently into his arms and began to move in time to the slowly seductive strains of a waltz. 'You're still as pale as a sheet, so don't tell me you weren't glad to be rescued from that worm's clutches.'

'I wasn't glad,' she insisted stubbornly, but honesty made her admit, if only to herself, that the gentle tempo of the music and Bart's arm reassuringly firm at her waist sent a soothing balm over her agitated nerve ends.

Local dances were never late affairs, and by just after eleven the foursome were installed in the car and being driven home competently by Bart, who had taken the wheel after a murmured conversation with Russ. After a little low-toned initial conversation at the rear, Patty and Russ lapsed into a significant silence broken only occasionally by whispered murmurs.

At the front, Regan glanced across curiously at Bart, wondering what effect there would be at Patty's transference of interest to Russ. But the ruggedly handsome profile revealed only concentration on the road ahead, even the full line of his mouth showing no trace of tightness. Although the light from the dash was faint, his hair still shone like a silver halo, and Regan studied him, as she had so often since his arrival.

He was so totally different from any man she had ever known. Without being inordinately vain, she knew that as a matter of course men, especially ones she had just met, were unable to hide their masculine leap of interest in her physical charms. Parrying their too obvious preliminary advances had become second nature to her.

But there was nothing of that in Bart's attitude. On the contrary, the very few compliments he had passed had been given with an underlying note of irony, as if he found her more amusing than attractive. The idea piqued Regan, and she reflected idly that it might be fun to challenge his immunity, to get under that sun-tanned hide and uncover the real man underneath. What she would do with him once she found him was something she had no time to go into then, for Bart, seeming to sense her scrutiny, turned his head and gave her an odd look, surprising her by his softly spoken remark.

'Don't be so anxious to play with fire, Regan. You could get burned beyond repair.'

Her mouth opened in a silent gasp, her eyes wide on the profile he had returned to the front. And while she marvelled in her mind at his ability to reach into her mind and know her thoughts she summoned up her most blistering tone, though mindful of the silent pair in the back.

'Now don't disappoint me by saying you're not equipped to rescue me from fire as well as all the other catastrophes in my life!'

'I won't be here, will I?' he observed quietly, pulling the car to a halt outside Patty's home. Still there was no movement from the rear, and Bart said with purposeful loudness: 'You two have exactly fifteen minutes to say goodnight at Patty's door. If you're not back by then, Russ, you'll have to find your own way home.'

Regan was amazed to hear her brother's somewhat dazed but docile 'Okay, Bart,' as he helped Patty from the car and disappeared into the darkness, Patty's breathless goodnight floating back behind them.

'You really enjoy manipulating other people's lives, don't you?' Regan threw at the averted profile and saw a wry smile touch Bart's lips.

'Not particularly,' he drawled, turning his head lazily to regard her. 'Some people just seem to need a shove in the right direction—Russ, for instance.'

'Russ?'

'Sure. Without my pushing him with a little of the green-eyed monster, it might have taken him a few more years to realise how he felt about Patty.'

Regan was speechless for long moments before she got

out: 'It was because *I* persuaded Russ to show some interest in Jess Hartman that Patty dropped you like a hot potato!'

She saw the slight lift of his shoulders as he shrugged. 'Maybe it was the combination of the two, so we'll split the credits,' he conceded magnanimously, and slid an arm along the back of the bench seat until her hair brushed the smooth wool of his sleeve. 'Now are you going to admit that you were glad to see me when I interrupted that passionate love scene tonight?'

Regan reacted to the soft insinuation of his tone by throwing her head back and glaring up into a face that was suddenly much closer to hers. 'Certainly not! I could have handled Will Deighton this time.' Immediately the qualifying words were out she regretted them.

'This time?' he caught her up on them. 'You mean there was a time when you couldn't handle him?'

'That was when I was eighteen,' she scorned. 'I'm a big girl now, or hadn't you noticed?'

'I noticed,' he drawled, his eyes making a lazy inspection of the soft rise of flesh partially revealed by the scant folds on her flame-coloured dress. 'What you're wearing—or rather not wearing—is enough to inflame any man's senses. Even mine . . . cousin.'

The bending of his head was a mere silver flash in the moonlight bathing the front seat, his lips shocking in their warmth against her skin as he impatiently slid the silky material away from it. Agony tinged with unknown ecstasy pierced the numbed shock that deadened her senses as his mouth by turns nuzzled, urged, cajoled. Even while she moaned an apprehensive 'No, Bart, no,' an unhibited layer of her mind claimed the rightness of these feelings he aroused.

His head lifted then, leaving a trail of kisses like fiery brands across her shivering flesh. Regan's widened vision was filled with the polished gleam of his blond hair, with his strongly formed jaw and mysteriously darkened eyes that went over every detail of her hair and face and came to rest on the startled parting of her lips.

'You're too damn beautiful for your own good,' he muttered harshly, and crushed her to him with biting hands at her shoulder and back, his mouth possessing hers with the hard urgency of a man roused to passion against his will.

A dizzy kaleidoscope of colours whirled wildly behind Regan's closed lids as Bart's breath, warm and sweet, filled her mouth. Her hands spread on the wide implacable chest in an instinctive defensive motion, a panicked repudiation of the painful churning that began in the depths of her stomach and spread like molten lava up through her body until she was clinging with desperately meshed fingers to the white front of Bart's sweater.

His head lifted away from her slightly and his eyes raked the paled contours of her face and her eyes when her lids fluttered open over a puzzled glitter. She hadn't wanted him to stop. For the first time in her life, she knew what it was to desire a man in the same way that he desired her. The physical ache her body throbbed with could be assuaged in only one way . . . the ultimate way between a man and a woman.

Shock rippled through her when Bart thrust her away and turned back behind the wheel. He waited until the harsh unevenness of his breathing had levelled out before speaking.

'I'm not going to apologise for that,' he said tightly. 'It's what you've been asking for—what you intended—ever since you put that dress on tonight.' His head flicked contemptuously towards her. 'You and Russ planned it all, didn't you?'

Regan's mouth dropped open unbecomingly, though she told herself a moment later, as the warmth he had created ebbed slowly from her limbs, that his perspicacity should no longer astonish her.

'I—I——' she stumbled wretchedly, looking away from the accusation in his level look.

'You I can understand, but Russ . . .' He shook his head.

'God knows I'm no saint, but I'd draw the line at exposing my sister to other men's lechery in order to keep them away from a woman I wanted for myself!'

Regan's head jerked round to his, her breath drawing in on a harsh gasp. Was that all it had been on his part?—lechery? Was it possible that a man could rouse such feelings of passion mingled with tenderness, a longing to please and satisfy, without feeling something of that side of it himself?

She started when the door beside her opened suddenly and Russ's exuberant voice said at her shoulder: 'Slide over, Sis, and let me in.'

Her brother seemed not to notice the icy silence emanating from the figure at the wheel, absorbed as Russ was with his new-found happiness. Regan, however, was acutely aware of Bart's firmly clenched hands on the wheel as he drove speedily back to the ranch. The occasional brush of his sleeve across her skin, the muscled warmth of his thigh pressed to hers in their enforced proximity, sent tremors rippling through her.

'I'll put the car to bed,' Russ offered when Bart swung round in front of the house, and it was only when Bart, with a curt 'I'll say goodnight here, then', strode away to the porch steps, that he noticed something amiss.

'Something wrong with Bart?' he asked as he got in beside Regan at the driver's side of the vehicle. 'Is he mad because of Patty?'

'No!' Regan answered shortly, irritation rising to spill over her brother's head. 'He's mad because—I quote, "you exposed your sister to other men's lechery——"'

'I did what?' Russ yelped, bringing the car to a screeching halt inside the garage and turning off the engine before turning incredulous eyes on Regan.

'By asking me to wear something sexy so that Bart would be ogling me instead of stealing Patty from under your nose!'

Russ groaned. 'Why in hell did you tell him that?'

'I didn't have to,' she snapped, gathering her stole round her shoulders. 'He has a nasty habit of reading minds—very accurately most of the time.'

He was silent for a moment or two, then said sheepishly: 'I guess I shouldn't have said it at that. It wasn't necessary, as it turned out,' he added with a trace of smugness that made Regan's blood boil over.

'Oh! So now that everything's turned out peachy for you, you're willing to admit it wasn't a very gentlemanly—or brotherly!—suggestion,' she fumed.

'For the love of Pete, don't get on your high horse,' he returned impatiently. 'What lechery did you have to put up with when you were with Bart and me?'

'His for one,' she threw back tartly.

'Bart?' Russ stared disbelievingly at her. 'That doesn't sound like Bart, Sis.'

'He's a man like any other.' Her voice sank to a tremulous whisper. 'More so, in fact.'

'Regan? My God, you've fallen for him, haven't you?'

'No!' The denial sprang automatically to her lips, but one look at Russ's awed face crumbled her defences against the knowledge she had barely gained for herself. 'Yes—oh, I'm not sure. But don't you say a word to him, Russ Taylor, or I swear I'll never speak to you again! And you know I mean that.'

The threat, one of thousands she had levelled at him over the years, daunted her brother not at all, but his voice was gentle when he said quietly: 'Of course I won't say anything. But, Regan——' he paused delicately, '—Bart doesn't strike me as—as the marrying kind. He must have had hundreds of girls after him at one time or another, and he's still free.'

Regan fumbled with the door latch. 'Don't concern yourself about that, Russ. I'm the last one he'd take back to Australia as his wife.'

He caught up with her after switching off the interior light and fastening the doors to the garage.

'Maybe it's just as well, Sis. The thought of you living thousands of miles away in another country could finish Dad.'

'Dad doesn't have to worry on that score either,' Regan said lifelessly, and was glad of Russ's affectionately casual arm across her shoulders as they walked to the house.

Regan kept to her room the next morning until long after the men had left the house. Even on Sunday there were chores to perform around the ranch at least until mid-morning, and Regan decided to postpone facing Bart by driving herself into morning church service at Rivertown.

Her emotions were still as scattered as they had been last night when she had more or less admitted to Russ that she loved Bart. Endlessly she had asked herself as she tossed on her sleepless bed if what she felt was love or just an overwhelming response to a very physical, experienced man, spiced with the unusual ingredient of knowing that he was indifferent to her apart from a surface attraction her low cleavage had instigated. And even that scene of passion in the car had been prompted by his anger at the trick she and Russ had planned for just that eventuality.

Martha, busy with early preparations for family Sunday dinner later in the day, raised her brows at Regan's chaste appearance in white long-sleeved cotton dress and wisp of a hat perched on the shining brown of her head.

'Worried about something?' the housekeeper queried as Regan crossed to the counter and pushed two slices of bread into the toaster.

'Worried? Why should I be worried?' Regan reached into a cupboard for a china mug and poured coffee from the ever-ready percolator on the stove.

Martha chuckled. 'The only times you go to church are when you're worried about something or if there's somebody there who takes your fancy—like that substitute preacher a while back . . .'

'Oh, don't be foolish,' Regan snapped, turning her back

on Martha's knowing look. The housekeeper's uninhibited jibes had been getting under her skin more than a little lately, but she knew that any complaints to her mother would just result in a gentle:

'That's just Martha's way, dear, she doesn't mean any harm. I can't imagine what we'd do without her . . . loyalty like hers can't be bought these days.'

'Where's Mother?' she asked now, swinging back to face Martha.

'Your dad had a restless night,' she said, 'so I guess she's sitting by him while he sleeps.'

'Oh. Well, I won't bother them till I get back—Dad isn't worse, is he?'

'No, just tired,' Martha said reassuringly, her brawny arms rolling out pastry for that night's pie.

Not long after, Regan was on her way into town, concern for her father fading as thoughts of Bart filled her mind again. Was it wrong to go to church when her whole being was washed with secular thoughts of the most basic kind? . . . when her flesh still tingled from a man's amorous seeking, her lips stingingly full from the pressure of his? Yes, she decided as she walked up the shallow steps to the simple frame church. God must have willed it that His creatures should feel this way about one another . . . the physical, the emotional, the spiritual blending together to make a perfect whole.

Patty smiled her surprise and slid over so that Regan could slip into the seat beside her, and the service started immediately so that there was no opportunity for even a whispered conversation.

Regan's mind wandered during the over-long sermon delivered by the elderly churchman who had administered the rites for births, marriages and deaths for longer than Regan had lived. Fancifully, she pictured herself a bride at that altar, making solemn vows to the tall, blond man at her side, the man she would love for always. She leapt ahead to the oasis of coolness and peace she would create for him in the Australian desert, the handsome blond sons and adoring daughters she would bear him . . .

She came back to earth with a thump when the sermon ended and there was a general scuffling of feet as the congregation rose to sing the last hymn. Her lips moved mechanically, soundlessly, as cold reality poured over her. Bart didn't love her, could never love her in a thousand years. He liked Patty's kind, gentle, feminine and serenely competent in household arts. Russ had had his fling with Regan's fun-loving type, but it was to Patty he turned for a deep and lasting relationship.

Outside, she refused Patty's invitation to stay over for lunch with her father, excusing herself on the grounds that she was concerned about her own father. At that moment, she couldn't bear to be the recipient of Patty's happy confidences.

The sight of the doctor's car outside the front door of the ranch house brought Regan to a sudden halt behind it. It must be her father, she panicked, her hands beginning to tremble, her face paled to unnatural whiteness by the time she raced across the porch and into the hall. Dr Mathieson was coming from the living room when she cannoned into him.

'Doctor?' she gasped, looking fearfully up at him when he took a firm grip on her arms. 'Is it—Dad?'

'Don't get excited now, Regan,' he said in his gruff voice which somehow soothed. 'Your father's had another attack, but he's come through it.'

'Can I see him?'

He nodded kindly. 'Just for a few minutes, he's been asking for you. But Regan'—he called after her as she started away—'don't worry him by showing him yours.'

Regan nodded and went on winged feet to the back of the hall where her father's room was, but then her steps slowed and stopped and she leaned her head against the wood panelled wall. How could she hide her anxiety from the father she adored and who knew her better than she knew herself?

She became aware suddenly of a tall figure looming up beside her and glanced up to see Bart's intent look into her face.

'Oh, Bart,' she whispered brokenly, 'I can't bear it if he——'

'Of course you can bear it!' The harsh coldness of his voice hit her like an icy blow in the stomach. 'For once, think about him instead of yourself!'

Regan stared up at his caustic expression, her breath a jagged rasp in her throat. How *dared* he imply that her concern was with her own feelings rather than her father's! Her head came up with an angry jerk.

'My father means more to me than anybody else in this world,' she gritted, 'including myself!'

'Then go and show him that by not blubbering all over him and making him believe he's on his deathbed!'

Regan straightened her shoulders and went towards the bedroom door, then turned back to say icily: 'I don't think I've ever hated anyone as much as I hate you, Bart Kingman.'

'Sorry to disappoint you, but that doesn't bother me one bit,' he drawled unconcernedly, but his mouth had tightened to what might have been anger as he turned away.

She stared flinty-eyed after his broad shoulders, wondering how in the world she could have contemplated, even in her wildest moment, marrying him or anyone like him.

Her shoulders lifting and straightening, she walked into her father's room . . .

CHAPTER SIX

HESTER rose from the chair beside her husband's bed when Regan tiptoed over to it, exchanging an eloquent glance with her daughter before saying with quiet cheerfulness:

'I'll go and make some tea while you're here, Regan.'

Regan swallowed a lump in her throat as she watched her valiant mother leave the room. Never by word or gesture would she let Phil know the depth of anxiety his illness caused her.

'Hi, honey,' her father's voice, weak but still steady, drew Regan's eyes to the bed where Phil lay and she bent to kiss him on both cheeks. 'Did you say one for me?'

'What, Dad?'

'A prayer . . . at church . . .'

'Oh.' Regan's brow cleared, then her conscience smote her. She had been so busy with her dreams of marrying Bart Kingman that the thought of praying for her father or anyone else hadn't entered her mind. Nevertheless, she lied blandly, 'Of course I did. I can't say it did much good, though, can I?'

Phil essayed a chuckle. 'God works in . . . mysterious ways, honey.' Unexpectedly he asked: 'What's it like outside today? I haven't . . . seen anything but this room.'

Regan swallowed and said softly: 'It's hot . . . so hot that half the congregation went to sleep during the sermon instead of the usual quarter.'

He smiled. 'That man always was too long-winded.'

There was silence between them for a moment or two, but Regan felt the flow of communication from the hand she held in hers.

Phil's eyes were growing heavy when he looked up at Regan. 'That dratted doctor . . . gave me stuff to make me sleep. Tell your mother . . . she's not to come back till I . . . wake up. Had enough . . . this room for now . . .'

Regan stayed with him until he slept peacefully, his breathing regular though light. Tears stung her eyes as she bent to kiss his forehead, tears she had been able to stem while he was conscious, thanks to Bart's needling before she entered the room. Without that, she would have broken down as she had at her father's first heart attack, a circumstance that had done nothing to help his recovery.

She went quietly out and across the hall to the living room, stopping involuntarily when Bart's drawl came to her clearly.

'Well, I think you're wrong, Aunt Hester, but if it's what you want——'

'More importantly, it's what Phil wants,' she interrupted, quietly firm. 'I've no intention of going against his wishes now.'

'What wishes?' Regan asked starkly from the doorway.

'Regan! I thought you were with——'

'Daddy's asleep.' Then, as if the childish name for her father had broken her tautly held spirit, Regan's lip quivered and in another moment she was being enfolded in her mother's comforting embrace, missing the significant look that passed from Hester to Bart and Russ.

'I must go to him,' Hester said gently, and Regan pulled away, accepting the man-size handkerchief Russ put into her hand and dabbing at her eyes before blowing her nose and sitting down on a chair arm.

'He—he said you're not to go back till he wakes up,' she sniffed. 'You've had enough of that room for now, he s-said.'

'Dad's right, Mom,' Russ put in before Hester could protest. 'I'll go and sit beside him for a while.' He patted her shoulder as he passed. 'Don't worry, I'll call you if there's any need.'

When he had gone, Regan sat up straight and looked at her mother. 'How bad is he? The doctor said——'

'It could have been much worse if your father hadn't been

taking a lot of care lately,' Hester replied, then glanced at Bart, who sat on one of the deep curved chairs near the window, his expression unreadable. 'The doctor wants your father to go to Vancouver for more tests, Regan.'

'When?'

'As soon as he can arrange transportation.' She looked hesitantly at her daughter. 'Probably tomorrow.'

Regan rose purposefully, glad of something concrete to do. 'Then I'll pack the things we'll need so we'll be ready when the time comes.'

'No, Regan!' Hester's voice was sharp with strain. 'Only your father and I will be going.'

Regan stared at her bewilderedly. 'But why?'

'Because there's nothing you can do, dear, and—because that's what your father wants.'

'Dad doesn't want me there?'

'It's not that he doesn't want you, darling, it's just that——'

'He's undergoing perfectly normal tests,' Bart put in levelly from the chair, 'so it's unnecessary for anybody but your mother to be there. If you insist on going, he's going to think he's a lot sicker than he really is. It's much better that you do as he suggests.'

'And do what? Bite my nails to the quick?'

'Your father has made a good suggestion, Regan,' Hester said nervously. 'As you know, Bart's time is running short and he hasn't yet seen the stock he came here to evaluate. Dad thought it would be a good idea if you were to go with Bart, be his guide . . .'

'Me?' Regan's eyes widened incredulously. 'Why can't Russ take him?'

'Russ has to take care of things here, and the men are going to be busy branding, so you see, dear, there's no one but you to guide Bart.'

'He can guide himself!' Regan tossed back angrily.

'Oh, Regan, don't be difficult now of all times,' Hester

said dispiritedly, and moved to where Martha had appeared at the doorway.

'I'm sorry to bother you, Mrs Taylor, but Tom says he has to see Russ right away.'

'All right, Martha, I'll get him.' Hester cast a hesitant look behind her at the indignant Regan, then sighed and went out after Martha.

Regan heard nothing of Bart's rising or progress across the room until she was grasped by the shoulders and spun round to face his blazing eyes. His fingers dug like steel rods into her shoulders, and relief was shortlived when he lifted them from there and encircled her neck with determined pressure.

'Nothing would give me greater pleasure at this moment than to wring your selfish little neck!' he groaned through savagely clenched teeth. 'You've never in your life had an ounce of consideration or compassion for another human being, not even your own mother!'

Regan's face was slowly reddening as his fingers pressed against her windpipe, cutting off air to her gasping lungs, and she felt real fear streak through her. Bart looked uncontrolled enough to do what he threatened, and she knew she would be powerless to stop him. If only Russ would look in on his way outside!

A red haze began to blur her vision, and her fingers reached out in panic to clutch his shirt front, a drowning gurgle coming from her throat.

He let her go then, abruptly as if he doubted his own ability to control the passion driving him, and Regan fell back on the sofa, gulping the air that blistered her throat.

He leaned over her and said with distinct grimness: 'You're coming with me, even if I have to tie a rope round my waist and drag you!'

'I—wouldn't go—with you if—my life—depended on it!' she whispered hoarsely.

'Your father's life could depend on you doing as he asks,' he whipped back unmercifully. 'Don't imagine for one minute that I wouldn't rather find my own way. The only reason I'm taking you along is because I like and respect your father, and if having you out of his hair makes him happy then I'm prepared to put up with you.'

He stalked from the room then, leaving Regan a fuming mass of resentment at his high-handedness. But when she saw her father later that day, after the doctor had informed them that an air ambulance would be taking him to Vancouver the next morning, she knew she had no choice but to go with Bart.

'I'm glad you're going with Bart, honey,' he said weakly as she sat by his bedside while her mother ate a delayed dinner. 'He's been of more help than I could ever repay since he came here, and I know he can't stay on indefinitely. I'd like one of the family to guide him to the summer ranch so that he can see our new crossbreed in action. You know the country like the back of your hand, honey, and it's better you have something to do instead of sitting around here worrying about me.'

'I could come with you, Dad,' she pleaded softly, but he shook his head and smiled wanly.

'There's no need, chicken. One woman fussing around me is all I can take . . . where your mother's concerned, that's six females.'

So Regan put a brave face on it the next morning when the ambulance despatched by Dr Mathieson drew up before the substantial ranch house and Phil was installed comfortably inside.

'I love you, Daddy,' she whispered, kneeling beside the stretcher bed and kissing the side of his face.

'I know, honey, and that goes for me too, in spades.' Phil essayed a smile. 'I'll be back before you know it.'

'Promise?' she asked unsteadily.

'Promise,' he affirmed, a twinkle beginning in his eyes. 'By the time the doctors get through with me, I'll be better than new!'

The attendant reminded her then that the plane was

waiting for them, and Regan stood up, turning to hug her mother speechlessly before descending, her eyes blinded with tears, from the ambulance. It was Bart who helped her down, his arms that held her briefly, comfortingly, against his hard body as the steps were stowed away and the ambulance moved slowly down the driveway.

When the white vehicle had eventually faded from view, Regan realised that the arms still holding her were Bart's and she moved out of them with an involuntary jerkiness.

'When—when do you want to leave?' she asked stiffly.

'Joe's loading up supplies right now,' he returned briskly. 'As soon as you've had breakfast we can leave.'

'I'm not hungry,' she said distantly, and turned to mount the steps into the house, his tone of command halting her before she was halfway.

'Nevertheless, you should eat. It may be some time before we stop.'

'Bart's right, Sis,' said Russ, coming up the steps and putting a supportive arm round her, his face showing signs of the same distress that marked Regan's. 'Fainting from hunger isn't a good idea when you're on a horse.'

'I'll tell Martha to prepare something for you,' Bart said over his shoulder as he strode past them.

'Oh, Russ, do I have to go with him?' Regan whispered, her eyes almost fearful on the broadly confident shoulders as they disappeared into the kitchen.

'It's better that you do, Sis. You'd just start worrying yourself about Dad if you stayed here, and that wouldn't do anybody any good.' He looked quizzically down at her. 'Changed your mind about him? I thought you'd jump at the chance of spending a few nights under the stars with him.'

'Never!' Regan shuddered. 'You don't know him like I do, Russ. He even tried to choke me to death last night to make me go with him.'

Russ shook his head. 'Regan,' he said with drawn-out exasperation, 'your sense of drama is getting the better of you again. Why should he want to choke you to death?'

'Because I said I wouldn't go with him.'

'That's why he tried to choke you to death?' Russ said incredulously.

'I said it in front of Mom, and she was upset,' Regan admitted honestly.

'Oh.' Russ pondered that for a moment before turning away to the front door, pausing to look back and say: 'I'll check that Joe's packing everything you'll need. And I'll tell you one thing, Regan—if Bart Kingman had really wanted to throttle you, nothing on earth would have stopped him!'

Regan stared after her brother for several moments before wandering towards the kitchen, where Martha, on Bart's orders, had filled a pan with thick bacon and yellow-yolked eggs.

'I can't eat all that,' she protested pettishly when the housekeeper placed a brimming plate in front of her at the kitchen table.

'Boss's orders,' Martha returned tranquilly, returning with the percolator to fill Regan's cup.

'Boss?' Regan bridled. 'What boss?'

'Bart, of course. Isn't he the boss of the mule train you're driving out today?' Martha, a staunch fan of television Westerns, chuckled hugely.

'He's not *my* boss!' Regan snapped, angrily attacking the bacon as if it was Bart Kingman's flesh.

The housekeeper moved comfortably over to where she was packing a canvas sack with food supplies for the camping pair. 'He comes the closest to it of any of the fellers who've been hanging around you.' She looked archly at Regan, her grin widening. 'Just imagine how romantic it's going to be, just the two of you in the middle of nowhere, sleeping side by side under the stars.'

'You and Russ have stars on the brain,' Regan said sourly. 'My sleeping bag won't be anywhere near his if I can help it!'

'Oh? You've suddenly lost your fear of bears and wolves in the hills?'

It had long been a family joke that Regan insisted on being the centre one of the three round the campfire when she, Patty and Russ had spent nights out of doors a few years before.

'I'd sooner face a grizzly than Bart Kingman any day,' she said bravely now.

'Not me,' Martha declared emphatically. 'Give me a hunk of man like Bart to cuddle up to any time.'

'Maybe you should be going instead of me, then,' Regan returned waspishly, rising from her half-eaten breakfast. 'I'd rather cuddle a rattlesnake!'

'He said you were to check the food and bedding,' the housekeeper offered to her retreating back.

'He can do it himself. Anyway, Russ is already checking the pack horse.'

'I'd better get this food out to him, then,' said Martha, shaking her head and looking thoughtful when Regan shrugged and went out without a backward glance.

Later, her features set in a stony mask after a farewell hug, more intense than usual, from Russ, Regan mounted her own Ladybird and took up a position in the lead of Bart and the pack horse following behind his mount. Bart had been given, or had chosen, a bay gelding befitting his own size, and his figure was indolently melded to the saddle as if he were one fluid part of the gleaming flanked horse beneath him. The front of his beige bush shirt was opened almost to his waist in deference to the sun already beating firecely down from a cloudless blue sky, his eyes shaded by the similarly coloured wide-brimmed hat he had pulled down over his forehead.

Regan, her own white smaller sized hat perched atop her head, her light brown hair a thick screen against the sun's rays on her neck, became uncomfortably aware of his level-eyed stare on the back of her plaid shirt and hip-hugging jeans. It was something of a relief, therefore, when he drew up alongside and cast her an enigmatic look from narrowed green eyes.

'Don't you think that as we're to spend quite a lot of time together in the next few days, we should at least try to be civilised with one another?'

'I thought acting in a civilised manner might be far beyond your capability,' Regan answered stiffly, pulling Ladybird's head sharply to the right when her leg brushed the taut beige of his.

Bart said nothing for a few moments, seeming intent on guiding his mount through the narrowness of a culvert which opened out to a wide panorama of sage-covered hills.

'I'm sorry about—what happened yesterday,' he apologised quietly without looking at her again. 'Believe it or not, I don't generally go around threatening to strangle women. I just saw red when you acted like a spoiled brat instead of the helpful daughter you might have been to your parents.'

'It's none of your business,' Regan told him in a low, furious voice, 'but I happen to love my parents—both of them—very much. So does it surprise you that I wanted to be with them right now instead of traipsing over isolated country with you?'

'It doesn't surprise me,' he admitted, surprising her, 'but you knew it was what your father wanted, and you were adding to your mother's distress by refusing to follow his wishes.'

'And I suppose you walked away from your sick father,' she jeered, the blazing amber of her eyes meeting the cool green of his.

'I had to walk away from my father knowing he was dying,' he said with an odd harsh intensity. 'There was a station to take care of, a family . . . I was the only one capable of doing it at that time. I never saw him again.'

Regan's breath had been held in abeyance while he spoke, but now it was released in a gasping sigh.

'I'm sorry,' she said, chastened. A bare glance at the grim outline of his profile was enough to tell her that he had suffered then, suffered deeply. And then a strange feeling came over her, as if she could see inside the make-up of this man and know what made him tick. He had loved his father deeply, that much was obvious, but he had found the strength to leave the dying man because of the sense of duty embedded in his deepest nature. He had taken his responsibilities seriously at an early age, and duty would always come first with him. The familiar drawl came to her again, and she saw that his eyes were fixed on the distant greenish-blue sage hills, though she felt that instead of the Canadian cattle country spread out before them, he saw the brilliant, more vivid colours of his own land.

'Strange,' he mused in a voice so relaxed as to be hypnotic in its effect, 'I found there were all kinds of things I wanted to talk to him about, ask him about, when it was too late.'

'About the ranch—station?' Regan asked, a quick rush of sympathy negating her previous antipathy. It was the most human Bart had shown himself, and in a way she could readily appreciate. There were so many things she would regret not having said if her father . . .

'No,' he drew her attention back to him, 'he'd already shown me all there was to running the station. It was more of a personal thing.'

Regan held her breath, feeling that if she kept quiet Bart might reveal more about himself than he had before. Nevertheless, she was unprepared for the shock his next words sent through her.

'I wanted to ask him things like: "How do you know, like you knew when you met Mum, that you've found the only woman in the world for you? Would you choose the one who's quiet, tender, gentle, or another who makes your blood sing every time she's near you, yet who maddens you so much you could cheerfully—strangle her?" He was the only one I could talk to like that, yet I never did.'

Regan kept her eyes strictly to the front, but she was aware of the slanting look he sent her through half-closed mocking eyes. Her thoughts were thrown into sudden confusion by his quietly spoken words. The woman he cheerfully wanted to strangle had to be herself . . . since the day before's episode when she had felt the hard pressure of his fingers against her windpipe she had known him capable of doing just that, but the rest of his description . . . Could it be possible that she was the woman who made his blood sing when she was near him?

A covert glance at his relaxed yet guarded profile told her nothing, and she realised with a tug of surprise that, even if Bart was madly, passionately in love with a woman, she would never know unless he put it into words. And that he would never do until he was absolutely certain.

'Well?' he asked, smiling amusement in his voice. 'What do you think he would have advised me to do?'

Regan's hand tightened on the reins so that Ladybird dropped behind a few paces. 'I wouldn't know,' she said stiffly. 'How could I? I never met him. I guess——' she hesitated, frowning, '—he'd have chosen the same type as your mother, whichever that was.'

The smile became a chuckle. 'Definitely the latter category, then. They struck sparks off each other occasionally in an almighty row and Dad would storm out of the house swearing like mad that if he didn't love that woman so much he'd do something drastic to her. Then he'd ride off by himself somewhere to cool off, and we'd hear no more about it until the next time.'

Regan, who had never heard her parents raise their voices to each other, stared at him bewilderedly. 'Didn't you mind it?—the quarrelling?'

'Mind it?' he echoed, equally bewildered evidently. 'No, of course not. It was their way of sustaining the love between them. I imagine the making up was just as passionate as the falling out.'

Warm colour bathed Regan's cheeks, heat that had little to do with the hot sun beating down on them. She had never before heard anyone, girl or man, discuss their parents' marital relationship at all, let alone Bart's casual acceptance of the more intimate details of it.

For once in her life, Regan found herself at an embarrassed loss for words, and after a glinting look of mockery that took in the revealing pinkness of her cheeks, the firm-mouthed averting of her head, Bart smiled and lapsed into silence too.

Regan became suddenly aware of the pungent odour of sage crushed under the horses' hooves, the pinks, reds, gold and yellow of wild flowers mingling their scents with the sage to create a heady fragrance that spiced her alerted senses. Ahead, shimmering in a mirage-like haze, lay the higher hills and rock-faced cliffs where they would spend their first night.

The thought of the night ahead sent an anticipatory shiver across Regan's skin, despite the still heat of noon that moistened the nape of her neck and the valley between her breasts to trickling wetness. Bart had moved slightly ahead again, and she scarcely had to move her eyes at all to see the long length of his firmly packed body relaxed comfortably in the saddle, the high polish on his boots already filmed with dust. Powerfully muscled thighs led to narrow hips and waist, which in turn flared out to a masculine breadth of shoulder. Little of the silver-blond hair could be seen under the wide-brimmed hat shading the deeply bronzed neck.

Regan admitted ungrudgingly that he had a basic kind of attraction that would appeal to the primitive streak in most women. And that's what it had to be with her, too. Nothing else about him appealed to her, she thought grimly, recalling with a shiver the vicious hardness of his fingers at her throat. Even his kisses had held little tenderness in them, for all her own urgent response to them. Something that wouldn't happen again, she determined as Bart pointed up ahead to where a stream meandered through a lightly wooded area.

'We'll stop for lunch there,' he informed her with no trace

of seeking her agreement.

Regan fumed inwardly, but said nothing because she knew that the idyllic spot would be the best stopping place for some miles, offering as it did shade and clear running water for human and animal alike.

It had been a long time since she had ridden so far without stopping, and Regan was stiff when she swung down from Ladybird's back, hobbling slightly as she led the eager mare to a spot downstream. Bart unburdened the pack horse of some of its load and took that and his own to plunge velvety nostrils into the cooling stream.

Regan took her towel from her saddlebag storage of toilet articles and knelt beside the stream to splash water on her face and neck, gasping when its chill took her breath away but glorying in the instant cooling over her entire body. When she straightened, patting at her skin surfaces to dry them, she saw that Bart knelt not far away sluicing his entire head and neck. When he rose, dripping, she tossed her towel at him.

'Here, we might as well wet just one towel for now.'

'Thanks.'

By the time he came to where she had laid out the sandwiches Martha had prepared, his hair darkened by the water and slicked back with a comb, she was able to toss off lightly: 'There's a thermos of coffee here, and another of some vile-looking liquid of doubtful origin.'

Bart chuckled, pausing to spread her towel on a nearby shrub before saying: 'Tea! I've been teaching Martha how to make it, and she produces a quite reasonable brew now, though it won't taste anything like the real thing over a campfire.' He surveyed their surroundings with a satisfied air.

'As long as you don't expect me to make it for you,' Regan said disdainfully, then bit into the melting tenderness of a sandwich made from their own ranch beef. Nothing but flood, fire, or other disaster could quell her healthy appetite, not even the presence beside her of a man who, she admitted frankly, played havoc with her senses at times.

The man concerned lowered himself to the soft bed of pine needles beside her, his shoulder brushing hers as he shared the tree trunk at their backs.

'Not only don't I expect you to make it,' he said easily, helping himself to one of the hearty sandwiches, 'I wouldn't want you to. There's an art to making tea the right way.'

'I think I can bear to face the future without that particular skill,' she responded tartly.

'I'm sure you can,' he agreed laconically, 'unless you happen to marry a man who likes his tea brewed the correct way.'

'Tea isn't the life and death matter to North American men as it seems to be with Australians,' she said disparagingly, lifting another sandwich to her lips.

'No,' he conceded, then gave her a slanting sideways glance. 'But what happens if you marry an Aussie, or even an Englishman?'

Regan chewed thoughtfully for a moment or two. 'It's extremely unlikely I'll marry either, so this is a pointless discussion.'

'Yes, I suppose you're right.'

She wasn't sure if there was a faint note of regret in his voice or not, but she welcomed the silence that followed, companionable as it was as they watched the contentedly cropping horses nearby. The only disturbance in the pastoral scene was the constant flicking of the horses' tails in pursuit of elusive flies and the human hands raised occasionally on the same errand.

'Well,' she said eventually, 'I guess we should be moving on.'

'What's the hurry?' Bart queried, sitting up away from the tree and looking lazily back at her. 'We'll easily reach those mountains where we'll spend the night, so why don't we relax and take a siesta?'

So saying, he angled his long body on a sideways slant to Regan and settled back with his head resting on her lap.

The narrowed green of his eyes challenged the indignant and somewhat startled amber of hers, and almost disappeared when he smiled up at her lazily.

'What more could a man want? A shady spot on a sunny day, a full stomach, and a pretty girl to stroke his brow.'

The feel of his head, the weight of it against her thighs, brought a tight feeling to Regan's throat and gave a strangled quality to her: 'The only thing you'll find stroking your brow out here is an army of horseflies!'

Nevertheless, when his eyes closed, still faced in her direction, a wave of protectiveness engulfed her, her hand brushing gently at the occasional black-legged fly or persistent mosquito seeking sanctuary on the smooth-shaved side of his jaw.

Seeing him like this, his mouth still partly curved with his last smile to her, Regan could easily believe that what she felt for him was not wholly physical. A visionary world enfolded her as she looked searchingly down at him, a world of sun-filled days and passionate nights, of brown strong-limbed children with hair the colour of moonlight on a faraway Canadian lake . . . Sighing, Regan closed her eyes and leaned her head backward to the tree, her hand lying idly on the warm skin of his neck.

CHAPTER SEVEN

'You have hidden talents,' Bart pronounced later that day when they had decided on a spot to make their overnight camp. His eyes were lit with genuine admiration when he came back from unloading and watering the horses, hobbling them so that they would not wander too far during the night in search of the somewhat sparse clumps of grass scattered over the mountain side.

Regan, hungry from the long afternoon's ride, had arranged the keyhole campfire Russ had always used on their trips, rocks set narrowly at one end for the cooking of their meal, the wider circle intended for warmth during the cool mountain night.

'We'll need a lot more wood,' she returned crisply, 'and I can't find any matches in the packs. Do you have any?'

'You didn't check that there were matches before we started?' Bart queried, frowning.

'Russ said he was going to check,' she said, avoiding the kindling anger in his eyes by taking the steaks Martha had put in the canvas pack for their first night's meal. Meat which had to be cooked that night or it would spoil in the blazing heat of another day.

'It's always better if one of the party does the checking,' he said with an obvious effort at control, adding drily: 'They've more to lose if there's something missing. That's why I told Martha——'

'I don't take orders from you!' Regan snapped, rising from her crouching position to face him defiantly, though still at a grave disadvantage against his height.

'Oh, I see.' He contemplated her in silence for a few moments, his thoughts hard to read from his poker expression. 'Well, whether you like it or not, on a trip like this there can only be one boss—and that sure as hell isn't you!'

These last words he whipped out with all the cold rage of a man accustomed to being the unquestioned boss, particularly where women were concerned.

'If you're so damn clever,' she swore back at him, 'how come you need me along as a guide?'

'Not because——' Bart's eyes, fully open now as the sun's fierceness disappeared behind the high ridged mountains, flickered with an odd expression just before he lifted a dismissing hand. 'Bickering isn't going to get us anywhere. What would you suggest we do to get the fire alight?—rub stones together?'

'You're the boss,' she returned sweetly.

'Yes,' he acknowledged without a blink, his hand going to the breast pocket of his bush shirt. 'And as such, I always try to travel prepared for emergencies like this.' When his long brown fingers re-emerged from the pocket, they held a slim folder of matches. 'It's fortunate that when I gave up smoking I didn't lose the habit of carrying these around with me.'

Regan breathed hard. 'You've had those all the time, yet you let me think——?'

Unexpectedly, he chuckled and tossed the folder into her instinctively raised palm. 'Here. Now you can show me what a wizard you are with the cooking pots. By the time I get back from washing, you should have a delectable campfire meal ready.' His derisive laugh indicated his disbelief in that possibility, and Regan gritted her teeth as she watched him walk lazily over to his saddle bags and extract towel and toilet gear.

She wouldn't have minded a cooling wash herself, she fumed as she set light to the fire's kindling, watching with bated breath when it caught and flared up round the larger pieces of dried wood she found close by.

But she ignored the inviting sparkle of the stream when she went down to fill the water pot preparatory to soaking the dried vegetables she intended using for their meal. Harder to dismiss from her view was the sight of Bart, muscled torso bare to the waist, bent over and sluicing water over as much of his bronzed skin as he could reach.

Almost without thinking, Regan crossed quietly on the grassy verge and positioned the brimming pot over the clear outline of his spine, letting it fall in a stream from the height of her arm's length.

Disappointingly, his shock was more at her presence than the temperature of the water, and she reflected that it couldn't be as cold as she had expected. How wrong she was about that was revealed a second later when she found herself pinned with a steely arm to Bart's chest. Wetness and bone-deep cold transferred itself from his flesh to hers, and tautened her skin to tingling awareness of his maleness.

'That wasn't a very clever thing to do,' he drawled deceptively; his jaw had a definite firmness about it, his eyes deadened in their coolness. 'Now I'll have to retaliate, won't I?'

'Not if you want your dinner within a reasonable time,' she retorted with more bravado than she was feeling. 'I'd have to dry my hair and change my clothes . . .'

'Oh, I wasn't thinking of doing something as unimaginative as repeating what you just did to me.' His eyes travelled down to her lips where the lower one's fullness trembled very slightly. 'I can think of a lot more ways of extracting revenge, ways that would be much more satisfying to me.'

'I like being kissed, if that's what you mean,' she said with a bold uptwist of her neck so that her eyes met his, 'so it wouldn't be as satisfying as you think.'

His hand spread slightly on her spine and brought her even closer to the lean lines of his body. 'You like to be kissed, do you? By me, particularly, or will anyone do?'

Regan gave a little laugh, more breathless than she had intended. 'Are all Australian men as egotistical as you?'

His brows rose. 'Who's egotistical? A man doesn't have to be a bighead to know when a woman responds to his lovemaking.'

His eyes went slowly, lingeringly, over her face and rich cascade of hair and Regan knew that he was remembering, as she was, the few kisses they had shared. Suddenly, suffocatingly, she felt her heart leap into a poundingly erratic rhythm and knew that she wanted him to kiss her—wanted it more than she had ever wanted anything in her life.

She pressed back against his hand, away from the smooth coldness of his chest, where water still trickled down it, in the vain hope of hiding the excited thunder of her heart. A slow smile curved the outline of his mouth.

'You're quite a fraud, Regan Taylor,' he drawled softly. 'You react like a woman when you're kissed, but I'd guess that when you're faced with the passion you rouse so very easily in a man, you run like a scared rabbit.'

'I do not,' she choked childishly, struggling without success to free herself from his iron grip, then throwing impotently up into his face: 'I certainly wouldn't run from the amount of passion *you're* capable of!'

For a moment she felt a thrill of fear tingle along her spine as his jaw firmed, his eyes narrowed, but then he gave a dry laugh in his throat and released her.

'Go about your supper business, sweetheart, and thank your stars that your mother trusts me not to harm her precious daughter . . . in that particular way.'

He bent down to retrieve his towel, and Regan went stumblingly to refill the pot, making her escape seem just the thing she wanted.

And that was what she had wanted, wasn't it? she questioned herself as she soaked the dried vegetables beside the fire and turned to the steaks Martha had provided, seasoning them with an abstracted air. But what, then, had all that heart-pounding excitement been about while Bart held her implacably against him? A natural occurrence, she told herself firmly, when a girl was held that closely to a man's—any man's—attractively masculine body. She had admitted that Bart Kingman was physically attractive, and now she was honest enough to admit that he was probably correct in thinking she would be a scared rabbit in face of his particular passion. Despite her brave words, she knew that he affected her as no other man had ever done before.

The answer to that one was simple, she determined quickly when Bart's lean figure hove into view. He had changed into clean pale green knit shirt and cotton trousers, and held a pile of dry firewood in his sinewy arms. She would make sure that such a situation of close proximity didn't arise again.

'Keep an eye on the steaks, will you?' she asked briskly, rising. 'If I don't have my wash now, it'll be too dark.'

'Will do,' he returned, equally noncommittal. 'Shouldn't the vegetables go on too?'

'Five minutes.'

Regan took her toilet gear and clean blouse and made for the stream, revelling in its murmuring song over smooth rocks, its refreshing coldness against her heated skin. Yes, that was what she would do . . . keep a clear distance from Bart's disturbing presence all through this enforced trip. And not long after their return to the ranch, he would be leaving to go back to his own country. He would forget the Canadian scene, and she would forget him . . .

'Bart?'

Regan's voice quavered out of the fear that had gripped her for an hour or more. Schooling herself to lie some distance from the only other human for miles, she had set her sleeping bag at the far side of the fire from Bart's. Even his dry: 'I don't turn into a werewolf at midnight, you know!' failed to deter her from keeping the distance she had promised herself.

Sleep had claimed her in the beginning, but something had awakened her, some noise in the tree-clad hill behind their campsite. The awful thought struck her that they might have camped right on the path to water used by the nocturnal creatures prevalent in this country.

Another dry crack sounded clear in the night air and Regan started up with a stuttering cry.

'*Bart!* Please . . . wake up!'

Then, almost as quickly as if he had been awake all along, his familiar drawl came from the other side of the fire.

'Regan? What's wrong?'

'It's—didn't you hear it? Th-there's s-something out there.'

'What?'

'I don't know!' Sharpness brought about by the fearsome cold in her bones edged Regan's voice in defence against the half-amused tone in his. 'It could be a b-bear.'

'Rubbish! Any sensible bear would be fast asleep at this moment . . . and I'm beginning to envy him!'

In spite of her immediate bristling, Regan was strangely comforted by his matter-of-fact tone. 'It—it could be a wolf,' she offered after a short silence.

'Oh, for God's sake, Regan, if it *is* a wolf he'll be looking for a likely mate . . . which isn't you, delectable though you might be to man.'

Regan pondered these words for a short time.

'Be a good girl and go to sleep, for Pete's sake,' Bart said at last, his head and shoulders disappearing alarmingly between the down-filled contours of his sleeping bag.

Did he really think of her as being delectable? He had said once that she was too beautiful for her own good—and had shown a certain amount of controlled passion now and then. But he had made it clear on more than one occasion that there were many desirable character traits absent from her make-up, attributes more necessary in his eyes than any physical attraction she might have for him.

Half purposefully, she lost herself in that thought until another stealthy sounding movement penetrated her ears. By diving under the covers, she managed to stifle her involuntary cry, but a sudden long-drawn unearthly sound from a tree branch near by proved too much for her tautly strained nerves and she moaned her terror.

'Regan! Regan, it's only an owl,' Bart's voice, patient yet laced with fury, came from above her.

Her head ventured out of the bag and she looked up at the glint of moonlight in his eyes, the shaft of it lighting his bare torso.

'Out you get,' he commanded grimly.

'Wh-what for?'

'So that, with any kind of luck at all, I'll get an hour or two of undisturbed sleep!'

With a lightning bend and a quick flip of his wrist, he unzipped her sleeping bag and hauled her to her sock-clad feet, bending again immediately to pick up the bag and carry it across to the other side of the campfire.

Little heat came from the ashen embers, and Regan shivered in the cool clearness of moonlit night, her eyes widening as the sound of zipper pulling came again.

'What are you doing?'

Wincing when her unprotected feet contacted the sharp edges of pebbles surrounding the fire area, she hopped over to stare aghast at the sleeping bags, now cosily zipped together to make a double.

'I can't . . . sleep there with . . . with you!'

'Don't worry,' he told her laconically, 'my interest at this moment centres on sleep, not ravishment. You'll be as safe here as you were over there.' He held open the upper bag and made a mocking gesture. 'Get in and let's see if we can salvage what's left of the night. It should comfort you to know that whatever it is you're afraid of will get to me first.'

Whether it was because of his drily proffered invitation, indicating that his only desire was for sleep, or the certainty that he would install her forcibly if she demurred further, Regan gave in and stepped over to slide down at the far side of the mated bags.

It would still be possible to keep her distance, she assured herself, and his nearness would calm the terror that always gripped her in the vast outdoors with its strange night sounds.

Watching Bart's poker face as he bent to reactivate the fire, she knew that nothing could harm her while he was near. Nothing would dare! Not bear, nor wolf, or coyote . . .

Her breath seemed suspended when, after an almost unnoticeable hesitation, Bart lowered himself between the sleeping bags and zipped up the open end, enclosing them more intimately than she had anticipated. The feel of one wide shoulder against hers made her change her position to lie on her side facing him. Why hadn't he worn his shirt to bed, as she had? There was something almost indecent . . . sensual . . . about the closeness of tanned male flesh only inches away from her own.

'Bart?' she said tentatively after interminable minutes had gone by. His eyes had been closed at first, but now she saw the silver shaft of moonlight in their open depths.

'What is it now, Regan? Still scared?'

There was a note of weary patience in his voice, but his arms were gentle when, without waiting for her reply, he lifted her to lie alongside his long body and settled her head in the hollow of his shoulder.

'All right now?'

'Yes, but——'

'Regan!' he warned like a man rapidly reaching the limit of his endurance.

'I'm not scared any more,' she said, softly contrite, wondering if that was entirely the truth. Tremors of feeling akin to panic were running over her at the touch of his shoulder under her cheek. For all it was so leanly padded, it was a remarkably comfortable resting place. Warmth spread from his body to hers, comforting yet strangely disturbing.

'Then go to sleep.'

'I'm not sleepy any more . . . are you?'

An explosive sigh that lifted her rib cage as well as his broke from him.

'No,' he admitted tightly. 'Strange as it may seem to you,

I'm reasonably human. It's not every night I hold an attractive girl in my arms without——' His voice broke off abruptly, the arm he had curved round her slender frame loosening so that she became aware of the tension that had been in it.

'Without making love to her?' Regan finished for him, her voice husky with unknown emotion. 'Is it because Mom trusts you not to do just that?'

The answer to that last question was suddenly of great importance, as was evidenced by the deepened, almost sickening thud of her heart against his side. The knowledge was borne in on her that, out of all the men she had been amorously involved with, to greater or lesser degrees, there wasn't one she could envisage lying here with in such intimacy without feeling that old panic surge through her. It wasn't lack of excitement—every nerve in her body was aware of his potent masculinity—it was the shrinking away from that masculinity that was absent now. She realised Bart hadn't yet answered that all-important question.

'Well?' she lifted her head and twisted her neck to look at him.

'Your mother's only a small part of it,' he said reluctantly at last. 'I never start any project when I know there can be no satisfactory end to it.'

Crushed, she lay heavily back against his arm. In a small voice which unconsciously betrayed a note of childish petulance, she said: 'Why couldn't there be a satisfactory end between you and me, Bart? What if I told you I'd fallen in love with you?'

The words trembled in the air between them, Bart's breath seeming momentarily trapped in his chest. Then he said brusquely: 'You're not in love with me. You just want anything that appears to be out of reach, like a child screaming for another's toy.'

Silence descended, a thickly oppressive denial of the light air around them, but at last Regan's heart steadied enough for her to ask quietly:

'And are you? . . . someone else's toy?'

'I'm no woman's toy,' he answered, quick to anger on that point. 'I have—commitments in other directions.'

How cold, formal, it sounded! But why had she never really considered the possibility that a woman waited for him somewhere in Australia? As Russ had said, Bart must have had hundreds of girls showing a more than casual interest in him . . . was it so unreasonable to think that he had left a special someone back there? But then why hadn't he brought her with him? Such a trip as he had undertaken would have made an ideal honeymoon. Regan swallowed hard.

Already she regretted her suggestion that she could fall in love with him. The other girl, if she existed as one of his 'commitments', was welcome to him. Anyone who regarded love and marriage with such a cool eye could never be the man for her, Regan, anyway. Her only recourse now was to convince him that her remark had not been seriously meant.

In an obvious way, she moved from the shelter of his arm and shoulder and said flippantly: 'Well, I'm no nearer sleep than I was before. Tell me about Australia.'

For a moment or two he was silent, his eyes fixed on the blaze of stars above them, then his arms lifted to support his head and he said slowly:

'Australia's a big country, too big for me to know it well apart from the area I live in. That I do know well.'

'Then tell me about that,' she demanded lightly, turning on her left side to watch his face in the silver glimmer of moonlight warmed by the flickering sporadic flames from the fire. It was as good a subject as any to induce sleep, she reflected, and one guaranteed to divert Bart's mind from her own foolish talk of loving him. She must have been carried away by the romantic surroundings they found themselves in, her own psyche having been primed by Martha's fanciful projections. A wry smile moved her lips when she imagined the housekeeper's comments if she saw Regan now, alone on a mountainside in a sleeping bag with the half-clad Bart, under a star-studded velvet blue sky.

These thoughts flitted through her mind while she barely listened to Bart's soft drawl from close by. Suddenly her head jerked up.

'*How* big did you say your ranch—station—is?' she asked in high-pitched amazement.

'Over a million acres,' he returned casually, then turned his head in her direction. 'You have to understand, Regan, that in an area such as ours in the north-west, where droughts can happen several years running, there has to be a vast property to provide even minimal feeding for the stock.' His gaze returned to the night sky. 'When all the plans we have for irrigation get under way, the land should improve a lot—enough to support this new crossbreed herd I've come here to see.'

'You're not really poor at all, are you?' she put in when he paused.

'Poor? No. Rowanlee is one of the more prosperous properties in the area, and like most Australians I like a gamble and fortunately I've been pretty successful in the investment field.'

'Why did you let us think you were—well, not very well off?'

She saw the glint of his teeth when he smiled.

'It wasn't my intention to let you think we barely existed from one drought to the next, but you seemed to want to believe that I was—how did you put it? Small, narrow-shouldered and resorting to hornrims, and—poor. I hadn't the heart to prove you wrong on all counts.'

'Thoughtful of you!' Regan cogitated for a moment. 'And I suppose you don't live in a rickety shack in the middle of the desert either?'

He chuckled softly. 'I guess you could say we're in the middle of the desert by your standards, but the rest doesn't apply. The homestead is fairly rambling, good sized rooms with verandas all round . . . they're used as sleep-outs when the weather's hot. We have an adequate number of bathrooms and the other facilities that go towards making life as comfortable as possible.' His voice took on a nostalgic quality. 'The gardens are a dream, bright with tropical flowers and birds most of the time, and trees for shade where it's needed.'

He went on to talk about the animals and birds native to his part of the world, the white cockatoos, pink-breasted galah birds breathtaking against a metallic blue sky, and the 'bushman's clock', the kookaburra, which threw its head back at sunrise and sunset and laughed with an almost human sound.

'It sounds . . . different from the way I pictured it,' Regan put in sleepily at last, but then what was there about Bart that wasn't different from the way she had imagined? 'Would I like it there, Bart?'

He appeared to think for a moment, and her eyes were almost closing when he spoke at last. 'That's hard to say, Regan. It can be a hard country for a woman not used to it.'

'Your mother adjusted . . . after England.'

'Mainly because she loved Dad so much,' he said softly. 'Wherever he was, was where she wanted to be.'

'Whither thou goest . . .' Regan began to quote, but was asleep as the words left her lips. Apart from a rapid deepening of her slumber, she was unaffected by the gentle drawing up of the down quilt over her shoulders to a point just above her ears.

The stars were reluctantly giving way to dawn when she half roused and found herself reinstalled on Bart's shoulder. From the dry warmth permeating from his chest and encircling arms she felt an almost unbearable sense of animal comfort.

His mouth, firm and peaceful, lay a breath away from hers. She felt his breath warm against her skin, and the temptation to reach up and touch his lips with hers was more than her sleepy senses could deny.

Like a butterfly alighting on a flower, she brushed his

lips softly with hers, shockwaves jolting through her when his firmed and returned the kiss, his arms tightening unconsciously round her.

Her hand slid up to rest lightly against the short fair hair at his neck, feeling its male stubbiness, and, unaware of the pressure she was exerting to keep his lips moving sensuously on hers, she gave in to the sharply rising flow of desire flooding her limbs. Desire that swelled to block her throat and numb all other senses than the one that beat insistently along her thundering veins . . . his hand caressing the intimate curves of her body was as if designed for the task of arousing her previously unfelt deeper instinct to love and be loved, to submit with all that was woman in her to the dominant male's stronger passion . . .

Abruptly she became still, taking her mouth tremblingly from his. Was it possible that a man could make such love without being aware of it? Was Bart——? Her eyes flew to his face, finding the gold-tipped lashes still drawn over his bronzed cheeks. His breathing seemed only a little more rapid than it had been before, but through the clamour of her own heartbeat it was hard to tell.

Moving cautiously, she managed to turn over in the confined space and lay with her back to him. Tremors of guilt and shame shook her and brought weak tears to her eyes until she closed them tightly. Although she might lack many of the qualities Bart found desirable in a woman, dishonesty and stealth weren't among them.

If Bart had been aware, even half aware, of a girl in his arms, it was more than likely to be the one he had left behind in Australia, the one he had no doubt made love to in that particular way many times. There had been nothing uncertain in the expert caress of his hand, the sensual probe of his mouth. And that had been while he was asleep!—wasn't it? Perhaps he had been dreaming of that other girl, and Regan had simply made his dream more real.

But—*would he remember in the morning*?

CHAPTER EIGHT

THE sun was sending bright golden shafts over the mountain behind the camp when Regan woke again. Two sensations struck her simultaneously. One, that the air was cold as she struggled to sit up in the sleeping bag. The other was a sense of loss connected to the first. She had been nowhere near sleep after her shameful advances to the unwitting Bart when his arm reached for her and pulled her with possessive force to the curve of his body, his chin angling against her head so that her hair acted as a soft pillow for him.

She had hardly dared to breathe for a while, but then the warm drowsiness induced by their combined body warmth stole over her, and she had known no more until now.

Blinking the sleep from her eyes, she stared at an odd contraption dangling over the crackling fire in its circle of rocks. The teepee arrangement of branches from which to suspend a cooking pot was familiar to her, it was the smoke-blackened rough tin can hanging over the fire that held her gaze.

Her nose wrinkled, trying to discern what the aroma was that came from the slowly rising steam, and she knew with a sharp pang of disappointment that whatever the can held, it wasn't coffee. She had always loved the extra pungent odour brought out by the cool outdoor air, and she frowned her displeasure.

'Good morning,' Bart drawled from beside her.

She had been too absorbed in the contents of the mysterious can over the fire to hear his approach, but now she twisted her neck sideways and looked up at him.

His concession to the cold air had been the donning of his shirt and a dark green lightweight jacket, but it was obvious to Regan's sleep-soaked eyes that he had braved the icy water trickling down from the mountain. Perhaps entirely, she thought sourly, eyeing the clean unwrinkled cotton trousers covering his powerful legs.

'Good morning,' she returned frigidly, her parched throat crying out for a strong, hot brew of coffee. She waved a hand at the fire. 'What in the world is that thing?'

'My billycan of tea,' he said casually, going with a disgustingly fresh spring in his step to stow away his toilet gear.

'*Tea?*' she repeated, outraged.

'Nothing like it first thing in the morning outdoors,' he told her cheerfully, coming back to unhook the can and pour two enamel cups to the brim with the black noxious brew.

'You don't expect *me* to drink that stuff, do you?' she croaked as he crouched down and proffered one of the cups.

'I certainly do. Who knows, it might improve your early morning disposition!'

'There's nothing wrong with my disposition that a hot cup of coffee wouldn't cure,' she flared, finding her wrist caught and held when she made a gesture as if to tip away the rejected offering on the rocks beside her.

'Try it,' Bart insisted quietly and with just enough menace to make her look hurriedly up into his eyes. 'You can have coffee with breakfast, but meantime this is all there is to chase the cold away.'

They battled silently with their eyes for several moments, and Regan's were the first to drop. Shrugging, she lifted the unwelcome brew to her lips. At least, as he said, it was hot and liquid, and she could block off her sense of taste and smell as it went down.

Bart sat on the sleeping bag near her feet and regarded her quizzically as he drank from his own cup with evident satisfaction. A series of expressions flitted over her face as she swallowed. Distaste gave way to faint surprise which in turn changed to grudging acceptance that her empty stomach would hold the sweet black tea.

'Feel warmer now?'

'Yes,' she admitted shortly.

'Strange that the night can be so—torrid—at times, yet you can be frozen out in the morning,' he remarked conversationally.

Regan's hand jerked and spilled some of the tea on her blouse as she raised the cup to her lips again. *He knew!* He had feigned the sleep she thought was genuine, and was probably even now laughing silently within himself. But his eyes, her only means of telling whether or not he was amused, were obscured as he looked down into his empty cup.

Her throat, even if she had been able to find words to say, had closed over in a lump of embarrassment. She stared in stricken silence at the nervous movement of her thumb on the handle of her cup, which now rested on her lap.

Quietly, and with almost a note of gentle regret in his voice, he said, tactfully not looking at her as if he sensed her acute embarrassment:

'I think it might be best all round if we keep to our own sleeping bags in future.'

Sudden energy shot Regan to her feet and she felt none of the stones waiting to prod her feet as she leapt across the space to where her riding boots lay.

'That suits me just fine,' she snapped, thrusting one foot and then the other into the heeled boots and stamping on them until they fitted snugly round her instep before bending to tie the laces with trembling fingers.

'Regan,' he said, waiting for her to straighten up, her face red from bending. He had come to stand near, but her eyes refused to meet his. 'It isn't because——'

'Oh, don't be so damned stuffy!' she threw at him, moving away to collect her toilet gear. 'Hasn't it reached Australia yet that men and girls go camping together without being bonded by wedlock?'

'I suppose there are people there who think nothing of it, just as there are here,' he returned evenly, 'but I don't happen to be one of them.' He paused significantly. 'And neither are you.'

'You don't know that or anything else about me,' she tossed back over her shoulder as she headed stormily for the stream, 'and that suits me just fine too!'

Her words might have had more impact, she thought gloomily, surveying herself in a tiny hand mirror moments later, if her appearance had not been so unkempt. Her hair, tossed and tumbled round her face, had the look of a night really spent in lovemaking. She gave an inward laugh. Fat chance of that when Bart Kingman was her companion!

The day passed, long miles broken only occasionally by Bart's questions about the landscape, questions which Regan answered as briefly and succinctly as possible.

She longed now for the trip to be over. Even the sight of Bart's figure, lazily relaxed in the saddle, filled her with the stabbing darts of humiliation. The anger that burned inside her was partly for her own stupidity in initiating those intimate moments in the night. What had possessed her to leave herself open to rejection by a man like Bart Kingman, one she had been on a collision course with since their first sight of one another?

Her mind fastened on that word rejection. No one in her short and perhaps pampered life had ever offered rejection when she had wanted something. Least of all the males, from her father on down the line to Leo. She had been the one to spurn, to cast off.

That was it, she mused, glancing again at Bart who was chewing casually on the end of what had been a succulent stem of grass—a replacement, she suspected, for the cigarettes he had once used. His attraction for her must be because he was so different from any other man she had known, his indifference to all but her surface physical allure.

Lunch was a virtually silent meal taken in the shade of towering copper face rocks to one side of yet another valley, and by tacit agreement Bart made tea for himself in the revolting smoke-covered can while Regan prepared her own coffee.

'Where did you get that—that teamaker?' she asked suddenly when the food had been disposed of and they were lying back against the smooth rockface some distance apart. 'Don't tell me you brought it with you from Australia?'

He chuckled, losing a little of the aloofness he had maintained all morning. 'No. Martha produced it for me, and I've been breaking it in each time I've gone out with Russ and the men.' He eyed the utensil with some satisfaction. 'It's just about right now for making a decent brew. Martha also managed to find me some real tea—loose leaf, not the bag type,' he explained from under his hat brim to Regan's puzzled expression.

'Oh.' She was quiet for a few moments, digesting this. How was it possible that all this had gone on without her knowing a thing about it? Nothing would be too much trouble for Martha, even finding a billycan and real tea for him, enamoured as she was with his manly graces. Almost without thinking, she said: 'Do people around you at home run to do your bidding too?'

Bart eased his hat further over his eyes and settled himself more comfortably against the rock. His answer was less than direct.

'I get on well with most people, I guess.'

'Particularly women?' she asked caustically.

A lazy smile bearing traces of what Regan took to be smugness played around his mouth. 'When they don't disturb my sleep,' he qualified, adding with mock seriousness: 'And the Marthas of this world never do that.' The hat slid down to completely cover his face, and his voice came as a muffled drone. 'If you don't mind, Regan, I'm going to make up for some of last night's lost sleep now.'

And sleep he did, for a full hour until the sun reached round the cliff face and sought them out with fiery fingers. At first Regan glared balefully at his long-limbed figure stretched out comfortably, and fumed silently to herself.

The arrogance of the man! As if he had women lined up ready and anxious to make inroads into his well-earned male rest! But then looking at his easily placed form, one bronzed arm down at his side, the other across the rhythmic rise and fall of his wide chest, made her admit in honesty that it wasn't all arrogance on his part. There must have been many women . . .

But not her, not any more, she decided fiercely. So he was attractive . . . so were many other men, men who wouldn't spend their time pointing out all her faults. Men who would love her as she was, adore her, idolise her as others had in the past. On that note, Regan herself drowsed . . .

The spot they chose for that night's campsite—the last on the outward journey—would have been idyllic under other circumstances. The river they had followed most of the afternoon grew shallow and wider at a point between two hill slopes. High banks took a downward curve at that point to form a narrow strip of sand beach beside the murmuring flow. Bart straightened up in the saddle as if his back ached as much as Regan's.

'Looks like a likely place for the night,' he half questioned, his eyes taking in the natural clearing back from the river where there would be ample room for the fire and sleeping bags later.

Regan, to whom the place was long familiar from her camping trips with Patty and Russ, felt suddenly witchy and bent on thwarting him even in a small way.

'What about the horses?' she enquired coolly.

'I'll scout around and find somewhere for them overnight.'

As if supernaturally drawn, he led his horse unerringly in the direction of the patch of succulent greenery, nurtured by the shade of trees, fifty yards away.

Meanwhile, Regan slid wearily from Ladybird's back and went with her to the tempting water which, because of its shallowness, was tepid from the day's sun. It seemed cool, however, against the warmth of her skin. She had tied her hair back in a ponytail that morning and now she lifted the heavy bunch from her neck and dabbed the cooling liquid on her nape with a soaked tissue.

She was unpacking the supplies from the pack horse when Bart returned alone.

'There's a perfect place for them further up,' he said, lending a hand with the more bulky articles. He stopped then with one hand on the saddle blanket, his head cocked at a listening angle. 'What's that?'

'A waterfall,' Regan returned crisply. 'Russ and Patty and I have often showered——' She broke off, remembering too late that she was supposedly as much a stranger as he to the terrain.

The sharpened green of his eyes held a tinge of irritation. 'So why did you let me think you didn't know about the pasture over there for the horses?' He shook his head, his lips compressed to a tight line. 'Women,' he muttered, 'I'll never understand the convolutions of their child-sized brains if I live to be a hundred!'

At another time, Regan would have challenged his statement about the child-sized brains of women, but at this moment he was right. It had been childish of her to pretend ignorance, and it had accomplished nothing apart from irritating a man tired and hungry after a day's ride. So she went meekly to do his bidding when he told her to see to the other horses while he built a fire.

She lingered longer than necessary tending to the horses, but had to go back to the campsite at last. The fire, built in the same way she had done it the night before, crackled drily and sent spirals of wood-scented smoke into the air. Bart had spread out the sleeping bags to air on bushes edging the clearing and was now crashing somewhere back there in the undergrowth presumably collecting more firewood.

Regan quickly set about collecting the ingredients for their meal, getting water from the fast flowing river, and was stirring thick-bodied soup over the fire when Bart came back laden with firewood.

'Smells good,' he grunted, his back to her as he dropped the supply close by.

When he turned, Regan saw that his shirt, damp from perspiration from the day's sun, was also streaked with dust and clinging particles from the tree bark. He had removed his hat, and his hair looked damp too, his mouth and eyes edged with weary lines.

'Why don't you take a shower?' she suggested softly, sounding more wifely than she would care to admit.

'A shower?' he frowned, then his brow cleared. 'Oh, you mean the waterfall.' He came to stand over her. 'You must like the idea as much as I do—why don't you go?'

She shook her head. 'I can't leave this. I'll have mine later, or early tomorrow.'

'We can't be far from the summer ranch now.'

Regan kept her eyes on the simmering soup. 'No. We should reach it by noon tomorrow.'

'Well, there's no hurry to get there, is there? You can take your time in the morning, have your shower when there's some warmth in the sun.' He turned away to his saddlebag then, removing his toilet gear and clean clothes from it. 'I won't be long.'

Regan stared thoughtfully at his broad back as he disappeared in the direction of the waterfall. He hadn't really wanted her along on this trip, and she was sure he had been as anxious as she to terminate it. Why, now, was he in no hurry to reach the summer pastures and examine the stock he had come so far to see? It just didn't make sense. Her brows knitted in concentration as she removed the soup to a flat rock beside the fire and turned her attention to the beef slices in gravy which also came in dried form in a lightweight packet.

When Bart reappeared it was as a new man, and Regan envied his air of brisk invigoration from the stinging cold cascade that came from far back in the mountains, warming only slightly on its way to the river. The tan shirt and slacks he had changed into looked bandbox-fresh in spite of their mode of travel to this point, and even his eyes seemed a deeper shade of green.

'I feel like one of Macbeth's witches in comparison,' Regan quipped lightly, dividing the soup equally into metal bowls. It was true, she did feel hot and dirty as he came to share the smooth-barked fallen tree trunk. Her hair was still tied securely behind her head, but it nevertheless felt tangled and sweat-dampened.

'No man in his right mind would think of you in those terms,' Bart said with such sincerity that Regan's head jerked up in surprise, in time to see a whimsical glitter come into his eyes as he added: 'Especially when she's filling his very empty stomach with remarkably good food under less than ideal conditions.'

'These are ideal conditions for me as far as cooking goes. I hate being closed in by the walls of a kitchen.'

They ate in silence for some minutes, the thick soup hot and rapidly filling empty spaces within them.

'But you won't feel that when you have a husband and children to cook for, will you?'

It was more of a statement than a question, but Regan considered it gravely.

'I don't know,' she said slowly. 'I'm not like Patty, who just naturally gravitates to kitchens and domestic life. I'm—just a natural wanderer, I guess. The ties that bind aren't for me.'

Bart wielded a businesslike spoon on the last of his soup. 'That's because you've never been in love,' he stated firmly. 'My mother wasn't particularly domesticated either until she married my father, but it wasn't too long before she was holding her own with any of the other wives within a thousand-mile radius.' He chuckled, and accepted the dinner plate Regan silently handed to him. 'Now the reins will have to be pried out of her hands when I——'

'When you marry?' she supplied into the silence.

'Yes.'

'*Are* you going to be married, Bart?'

'Of course. Every man reaches the stage when he wants to settle down . . . a wife . . . children.'

'I meant——'

'Let's stop talking for a while and eat this before it gets cold,' he interrupted, a faintly jagged edge of irritation in his voice.

Conversation after that was limited and confined to less personal subjects. When the meal was over, Bart took over the dish-washing while Regan went further upstream to wash in the dimming light, promising herself a long cleansing all-over waterfall shower the next morning.

She made no comment on coming back to the clearing and finding the sleeping bags arranged for the night, close to each other but with a definite space between them. Brief anger spurted in her at the realisation that he felt a need to keep her at a distance as if he was helpless against any other advances she might make.

Bart Kingman helpless against any female! she snorted silently to herself as she slid between the downy layers which had been plumped to even greater loftiness by the airing Bart had given them. But other, more clear-cut thoughts passed through her mind as she lay sleepless on her back, staring up through the frond-like branches of the trees to the night sky above, hearing with part of her mind the gentle soughing of the breeze through the leaves, the closeness of river sounds as water continued to tumble over rocks.

No other man she knew—and probably most of those she didn't know—would have scrupled about taking advantage of the open invitation she had unwittingly offered Bart the night before. Yet he hadn't. Not because he was less of a man than they were . . . if anything he was more so. In that way, he had known Regan better than she knew herself.

There was nothing shocking to her in the sudden realisation that she wanted—needed—the security of a deep commitment on both sides when the moment of physical truth came. The reasons came thick and fast now for her hesitation over joining Leo in Central America, her tearful refusal to go out of her depth with Will Deighton, the others she had flirted lightly with and moved on.

Now, she knew, Bart was the one to whom she could make the deepest pledge there could be between man and woman, but she was realistic enough to know that she was driving on a one-way street where he was concerned. Still, she should be grateful to him.

'Bart?' she whispered softly.

'Mmm?' his voice came in immediate response, revealing that he was as far from sleep as she was.

'I—I'm sorry . . . about last night.'

'Don't be, Regan. Never be sorry about possessing very natural urges—as long as they're directed at the right person,' he added heavily.

Regan's eyes swivelled back to the sky again, her voice small and unlike her own when she said: 'And you're not the right person, are you?'

'No,' he said after a lengthy pause, then as if to mitigate the word's finality, added: 'If it's any consolation, *not* carrying things to their obvious conclusion was the hardest thing I've ever done.' He turned abruptly on his side, his back to her. 'Goodnight, Regan.'

'Goodnight, Bart.'

The fingers of dawn were barely reaching over the mountains the next morning when Regan, after sleeping fitfully, rose stealthily and busied herself quietly re-starting the fire and rigging up the teepee contraption Bart used for making tea.

While it brewed, she slipped off upstream to wash sketchily, remembering her later appointment with a shower. Back at the clearing, she drew a comb through her hair and decided to leave it loose until after her visit to the waterfall. Bart was still asleep, only his nose, eyes and sheaf of silver-gilt hair visible above the cover of the sleeping bag. However, one arm was outside the bag, as if in repudiation of the damp early morning coolness. He had kept his shirt on last night, Regan noted, and guided her thoughts away from the feel of his bare skin against her cheek the previous night.

Morning had brought acceptance of his brief acknowledgement that he wasn't the right one for her, but there was nothing to stop her pretending for the remainder of their little while together that here in the fastness of the mountains the rest of the world was closed out. That he would come to love her in the way she now knew she loved him.

She poured two cups of the steaming tea and sweetened them liberally before going over to his sleeping figure and kneeling there beside him. The hint of sadness in her light brown eyes lifted and disappeared as they went over what she could see of him. She loved the bleached white hair lying thick on his forearm, the sinewy strength it covered, the state of unawareness his closed dark-tipped lashes cast over his features, the nose that wasn't quite classically straight yet nonetheless proud . . .

'Bart,' she said softly, and saw his eyes open to immediate alertness. 'Tea.'

'Tea?' he repeated stupidly, slanting green gaze going from her face to the two cups in her hands. 'I must be dreaming.'

'I'm not entirely useless, you know,' she said crisply, pleased somewhere inside her that she had surprised him . . . pleasantly.

'I've never thought you were,' he said in a husky way that sent the blood tingling through her veins.

He pulled himself up to a sitting position and took the cup she offered, blinking in amazement when she moved over lithely to sit crosslegged on her own sleeping bag and lifted her cup to her lips.

'*You're* drinking tea without being forced into it?'

'It wasn't bad yesterday,' she conceded lightly. 'I could get used to it in time.'

His hair was improved very little from the fingers he ran through it. 'Where did you learn to make tea?' he asked suspiciously, eyeing the black brew.

'I've watched you make it enough times now,' she retorted wryly. 'Well, try it and tell me what's wrong with it.'

He sipped, then sipped again, his eyebrows lifting in true amazement. 'Nothing's wrong with it, nothing at all. In fact, it's good.'

His smile directly into her eyes was one he had never given her before. It lit up and narrowed his eyes to a light green glitter, sent youth to soften the sun-etched lines on his face . . . and made Regan's heart tumble over and over in her breast until she had to drag her eyes away and focus them dizzily on the water dancing over the rocks in the river just below.

Dear God, was this love? This pounding in her ears so that she heard nothing except the thundery beat of her heart, felt nothing but the ebbing of vital forces from her limbs?

Bart's voice came to steady her, as if he had free access to the innermost parts of her. 'Drink your tea, Regan. Where I come from, it's used as an antidote for all ills. Guaranteed to cure anything from acne to zinc poisoning.'

'Is that why you drink so much of it?' she asked without turning her head.

'Maybe,' he agreed after a barely perceptible pause. 'I used to think that men could control their destiny by sheer force of will, but now I know that's no more true than the faithfully held premise that tea cures all.'

Now Regan looked at him and saw the expression of thoughtful brooding on his face. 'You used to?—you don't think that any more?'

'That men control their own destiny?' He shook his head. 'I don't know, Regan. Perhaps it's a sign of maturity that I realise now that under certain circumstances sufficient force of will is hard to come by.'

'I can't imagine you ever being short of willpower,' she blurted without thinking.

He finished the tea in his cup before unzipping the bag and getting to his feet. 'I hope you're right, young Regan . . . I hope you're right.'

By his use of 'young' he had relegated her back to the position of younger sister, and Regan's smouldering eyes followed him resentfully as he stepped into his boots and headed for the river after collecting his toilet gear.

She would much rather be at the centre of a dramatic tug-of-war between his unbridled desires on one hand and his force of will on the other than be set aside as a too youthful spectator on the sidelines.

Unhappy with the turn her thoughts had taken, Regan shut them firmly from her mind and stood up abruptly, tossing the remainder of her tea into the bushes. Whatever curative powers it held for the Australians, its magic would never work for what ailed her.

Bart came back just as she was about to pour pancake batter into the pan. His wash had been thorough; the wetness of his hair, neatly combed now, testified to that, but he grimaced and ran a hand over his jaw.

'Have I time for a shave before breakfast?'

'I can hold back the pancakes for a while,' she offered, glancing at his seemingly smooth chin. Unlike a darker man, a day's growth of beard hardly showed on him.

'Thanks. I hate to sit down to a meal unshaven.'

It was quite a domestic scene, Regan mused idly, sitting back on the smooth trunk and clasping her knees with her hands. Woman cooking, man shaving as unselfconsciously as if it was a daily occurrence between a long-married couple. Again she switched her thoughts quickly from that subject, one that could only bring pain in its uselessness.

Bart had hung a mirror, larger than her own, on a twig shooting out from a nearby tree, and she watched as he ran the battery-operated razor over his jaw and chin, tautening the skin with the fingers of his other hand and contorting his face to reach awkward spots. A warm feeling engulfed her, a feeling that held the same cosy security she had always known as a girl when she had watched her father perform the same ritual. Her father . . .

'I can't wait to get back and find out how Dad made out,' she said with an unconscious sigh as Bart put the shaver away and came over.

'Made out with what?' he whipped, a cutting edge suddenly there in his voice.

'The tests, of course.' She stared up at him in surprise.

'Oh, yes. The tests. Well, I guess you'll find out soon enough.' His tone changed just as suddenly to one of lightness. 'Meanwhile, what about testing those pancakes on me?'

Regan lifted the frying pan without a word and reinstalled it over the heat. But all the time the pancakes were cooking, she mulled over his reaction to what had seemed a perfectly normal remark considering the state of her father's health. Did he think that, because she hadn't mentioned her father before, she had sloughed off all concern the minute the ambulance had borne him off?

It wasn't that way at all, but she forbore pursuing the subject until they had eaten the featherlight pancakes with an enjoyment known only to those whose appetites had been sharpened by early morning mountain air. Then she tried haltingly, while they sipped warm drinks, to tell him of the closeness she and her father had always shared.

'. . . I don't know, it's an uncanny thing in a way,' she explained slowly. 'I've often known, even when we're miles apart, just when he was thinking of me, and vice versa. It got to be a joke. It's something I can't really explain, except that—well, I don't have to talk about him all the time. I'd just know, inside me where it matters, if something was badly wrong with him.'

He slanted a sideways look at her. 'Would you? It's like that sometimes when two people care a lot for each other,' he said quietly, surprising her by putting a firm hand on her knee and leaving it there. 'You don't have to explain to me, Regan. I know you love your father, I've never thought otherwise.'

'Yet you . . .' she began awkwardly, then went on with a rush: '. . . When he had this last attack, you acted as if you thought I didn't care at all.'

'I hadn't much choice,' he smiled wryly into her eyes, then looked down into the fire. 'You were on the point of breaking down, and an emotional scene would have been bad for your father. I guessed that if I made you mad enough at me you'd forget the tears when you went in to him. I doubt if they would have helped Phil half as much as it did to see his daughter in control of herself.'

Her breath drew in on an astonished gasp. 'You did that purposely?' She swallowed noisily. 'I thought you were just being—hateful. Oh, Bart, I'm sorry.'

'My usual hateful self, is that it?' he smiled, removing his hand after a final squeeze. Regan missed its warmth at once through the thin cotton of her jeans.

'No, not as usual,' she said in a low voice, struggling against the helpless tears that clouded her eyes. 'I—I misjudged you, and I don't like to do that.'

'Oh, come on, Regan,' he said briskly, getting up and looking down at her bent head, a curious look in his eyes which she missed. 'I didn't think you were the weepy type. What I did was no more than I would have done—in fact, *have* done—for Vicky many times, so don't go all sentimental on me.'

There it was again, the comparison with his young sister! The very thought was enough to dry Regan's tears immediately . . . and restore her to the seesaw of conflicting emotions he aroused in her.

She blinked rapidly and stood up beside him, her shoulder several inches lower than his. 'I'll wash the dishes and take my shower.'

Bart stretched lazily so that the muscles flexed supply

along his shoulders and upper arms. 'What's the hurry? The water won't be warm enough by half yet—the sun's hardly reached it.'

'It won't make much difference when it does,' she returned crisply, pouring already heated water into the largest pan and beginning to rinse off their dishes. 'Anyway, I don't mind it.'

Bart lifted the towel and began to dry the plate Regan handed to him. 'I thought you didn't care for cold water.'

'I don't particularly. But I hate even more not being clean all over.'

'Oh.'

For just a moment Regan felt she could see into his mind, into the picture it had conjured up of her all over cleansing under the waterfall, and furious colour bathed her cheeks.

He, too, had obviously had a momentary glimpse into her thoughts, because he chuckled and pulled at a strand of her hair in brotherly fashion.

'Don't worry,' he teased, 'I never watch a lady bathe except by invitation.'

'And you've had plenty of those, I don't doubt!'

He seemed to consider. 'Not too many. Where I live, you see, there's a decided shortage of ladies I'd be interested in watching at their cleaning rituals.' His eyes lit up with an amused glitter. 'There is a lady in Perth, however, who——'

'I don't want to hear about her,' Regan snapped, almost throwing the last of the cutlery at him.

'I thought you asked me about the invitations I'd had,' he complained in a mock-injured voice. 'This young lady in Perth loves to have me around when she's taking her bath. She likes bubbles, lots of bubbles—do you?—In your bath?'

'I do not,' Regan gritted, emptying the pan under the bushes and wiping it furiously with a cloth.

'Pity,' he regretted. 'Bath bubbles can be very sexy.'

'You're obviously an expert on the subject,' she said frigidly, and stamped across the clearing to extract her last set of clean clothes from her saddle pack. Turning back to

Bart, she said curtly: 'You could clean up the campsite and saddle the horses while I'm gone, then we can make tracks for the ranch.'

'I thought I might take a hike up that hill over there,' he indicated the fairly steep rise across the river. 'Should be a good view from the top.'

'Please yourself,' she shrugged, and turned away.

As if he wouldn't do precisely that anyway!

CHAPTER NINE

THERE had always been something pagan to Regan in bathing under the waterfall, something primitive that pervaded her soul and body so that she forgot temporarily the world around her, the realities of everyday living.

The setting itself was enough to invoke visions of what it had once been like on the earth. Idyllic peacefulness, nature following her own course in the gentle fall of water from the ice peaks far from this spot, the pool edged with greenery it emptied itself into before trickling more slowly down to join with the river.

After the first breathcatching, heartstopping deluge over her still-warm skin her blood began to race through her veins, touching her limbs with icy fire. She stayed under the spray for a long time, exulting in the feeling of wellbeing that filled her body, but at last she stepped up and through the fall to the wide ledge behind where she had left her soap and small tube of shampoo. The latter she had not expected to use until that afternoon at the ranch, but her hair had felt as dusty as the rest of her.

Her surroundings seemed to lose their soothing quality as she soaped every inch of her body and rubbed the shampoo into a foaming lather on her head. Visions superimposed themselves on the tranquil pool and protective circle of trees and bushes. Visions of the woman in Perth, the one who liked Bart to be there when she bathed . . . the one who liked bubbles in her bath . . . the one who made herself sexy for him on his visits to Perth.

Even stepping under the waterfall again to rinse off failed to erase the pictures filling her mind. Was the woman dark or fair? Fair, she decided . . . no, dark to contrast with his fairness. Dark and voluptuous, that was the kind he would consider sexy. Her mind boggled at envisioning what transpired between them after the bathing ceremony.

She looked down to where the water sheeted over her tiptilted breasts. Definitely not voluptuous, she told herself regretfully. Nothing about her streamlined body suggested that appellation, no matter how many bubbles she used in her bath.

Her arms rose in a graceful gesture as if welcoming the water flooding her hair and face. Bart would go back to Australia and whatever it was that held him there, and she would forget him in time. A long time hence, there would be another man she could love——

'Regan!'

Her arms seemed to pull themselves down abruptly as the voice, which she suspected had called to her before, penetrated her consciousness.

'Go away!' she called back hoarsely to a Bart standing dangerously near at the edge of the pool. 'How *dare* you!' Her arms closed with an automatic gesture over her breasts.

'I'm not trying to be daring,' he shouted, his eyes seeming fixed on the wide-eyed stare in Regan's. 'Somebody's coming!'

'I—I don't believe you. Nobody comes up here.' Hot rage boiled through her, and without taking time to think whether such a motive could inspire the Bart she knew, she stepped back from the fall and threw her arms wide. 'You like looking at women in their baths, so look your fill! Sorry about the lack of bubbles!'

Away from the thunder of water in her ears, she suddenly felt the silence, apart from the tinkle of the fall behind her, stretch the short distance between them. Her heart tripped as Bart's jaw swelled to iron hardness, his eyes dropping only as far as the tautened rise of her breasts.

'Very nice,' he said in a voice dry with suppressed rage. 'I'm sure the boy scouts or whatever they are coming up the trail will be stunned.'

Confidence ebbed away quickly in face of his certainty

that people—boys—would be making their appearance at the waterfall any minute.

'M-my towel!' she gasped, and he bent stiffly to retrieve it from a spot not far from where he stood.

His eyes remained stonily on hers as she felt her way between the pool rocks towards him. Embarrassment had fled, to be replaced by nervous fear of his anger. Why had she done such a foolish thing? Whatever else he was, Bart could never be considered the kind of man to slink around staring at unclothed females.

And this was the gist of his harshly grated words as he draped the towel round her and pulled it tight over her throat as if barely suppressing a desire to strangle her.

'I've been called many things, but never a Peeping Tom! By God, Regan, I'd like nothing more at this minute than to slap your backside raw! And I might do it yet . . .' His head swivelled when the sound of excited boys' chatter came from the trees behind them. 'Get over there and hide yourself in those bushes while I head the scout troop off.'

Regan did, disregarding the sharp prick of pine needles on her bare feet, and huddled behind the thick screen of greenery, her teeth chattering now with cold. She heard the dull thud of Bart's boots receding along the narrow trail, then a man's voice, presumably the scout leader's.

'Hi there! I see you've beaten us to the waterfall this morning.'

'So it seems,' Bart drawled easily, as if he had not been a towering mass of rage moments before. 'My wife and I are camping a little way upstream . . .'

His voice faded to silence, and Regan presumed he had somehow reversed the progress of the troop. Nothing broke into the peaceful tranquillity surrounding Regan except the cool sound of water breaking on rocks and the drone of an insect near her head. She let out her pent-up breath in a long sigh of relief.

'My wife and I . . .'

The words echoed and re-echoed in her brain. Why had

Bart found it necessary to elevate her to wifely status? In this enlightened age, there were any number of appellations he could have applied—friend, partner, or even cousin, which would be closest to the truth. The answer was, of course, that he wasn't enlightened in that way. He was principled as he saw it, in the same way as her father was—which made her own asinine accusation even more reprehensible. Shivering, she waited for his return.

Minutes passed and there was still no sign of Bart's return. Maybe he wouldn't come back . . . maybe he was so filled with anger that he wouldn't trust himself to come near her until he had cooled off . . .

She dressed quickly, her skin dry now, and used the towel on her hair, rubbing it vigorously until it was barely damp. Unsnarling the tangles with her comb took longer, but at last she had no further excuse to linger. Carrying her boots and socks in one hand, her toilet gear in the other, she made her painful way back to the camp barefoot. The pine needles would best be removed if she had somewhere to sit in reasonable comfort.

The campsite was deserted, but Bart had to be around somewhere. The fire had been brought back to leaping life in its circle of rocks, and Regan welcomed its warmth as she hobbled over to seat herself on the fallen log and attack the worst of the jabbing needles. Absorbed in that task, her brows knitted in concentration, she heard nothing of Bart's return until he spoke from the edge of the clearing.

'What's wrong?'

She looked up, startled, unable to suppress the warm flood of colour to her cheeks. In his hand he carried the light fishing rod that had been strapped, unused, on the packhorse all through the trip.

'Did you catch anything?' she asked, avoiding his eyes.

'No,' he returned shortly, 'but I didn't expect to. There's a certain calming quality in casting a line, even over barren waters.' He propped the rod against a nearby tree and came to stand over her. 'I asked you what was wrong—what have you done?'

'N-nothing,' she stammered. 'I just have some pine needles stuck in my feet.'

'Hardly nothing,' he commented with obvious lack of emotion. The calming influence of casting had evidently sent his anger underground. 'I don't want to have to carry you around for the rest of the time we're together.' In one lithe movement, he squatted down before her. 'Let me see.'

'There's no need——'

'I'll decide that,' he dismissed brusquely, reaching none too gently for first one foot and then the other, frowning at what he saw. 'These have to be attended to or they'll fester.' A faint edge of irony entered his voice. 'I don't suppose you thought to check on whether we have a first aid kit with us?'

Mustering the remnants of her dignity, she straightened her back. 'Russ always packs a kit,' she said quietly. It was true. Lighthearted he might be in many ways, but Russ never forgot that one essential . . . not since Regan had had a bout with blood poisoning after gashing her arm on one of their trips.

'Let's hope he remembered it this time,' Bart said drily, getting to his feet and sauntering over to the supplies with only a faint movement of his hips. 'Any idea where it might be?'

'In a small canvas bag—inside that bigger one to your right.'

In moments he was coming back with the small square sack in question, lifting his brows when he drew out first a sewing kit for emergency repairs on the trail.

'Martha,' Regan explained briefly. The housekeeper felt almost as much horror over a ripped seam as Russ did for torn limbs.

'Well, let's hope we won't need either of them again.'

So saying, Bart knelt before her and lifted the most injured foot first. Using the tweezers from the kit, he pulled every one of the needles clean away while Regan gritted her teeth. Despite his almost tender clasp on her heel, the tweezers gouged with deadly accuracy on the sore points. Despite her determination to make no complaint, her breath drew in sharply when he painted the sole of one foot with red disinfectant before lifting the other to start on it.

'I'm sorry if I'm hurting you, but it has to be done.'

'It's all right.'

The other foot needed much less attention and was far less painful than the first. Regan unclenched her teeth and looked down at Bart. A frown of concentration grooved the area between his eyes and his lashes were dark gold arcs against his cheeks. As he dabbed on the disinfectant, strange feelings swept over her. Feelings that were difficult to classify . . . gratitude . . . tenderness . . . remorse. Most of all remorse.

'Bart, I—I'm sorry I said—what I said back there . . .'

He made no reply until he had replaced the bottle of disinfectant and tweezers in the first aid box and straightened up. Then there was only a terse: 'You'd better put your socks and boots on before something else gets under your skin.'

She blinked at the tears threatening to overspill from her eyes and did as he said, conscious of all his tallness standing over her while she complied. He didn't speak again until she had tied the laces of the second boot.

'Would you mind telling me,' he asked with deadly politeness, 'just what I've ever done to make you think I'm capable of doing such a thing?'

'It isn't what you've done,' she pointed out despairingly. 'It's what you said . . .'

'What I——?' He shook his head bewilderedly. 'What did I say, for Pete's sake?'

'The—the woman—in Perth—the one who l-likes bubbles . . .'

His jaw dropped in amazement, then a light of understanding, sparked to greater depth by a glint of dawning amusement, filled his eyes.

'Oh, I see,' he said softly. 'You mean the one with light brown hair piled up on her head, delectably round shoulders and dimples in her——'

'You are disgusting!' Regan hissed venomously, the nausea she felt churning in her stomach clearly reflected in her eyes. 'I take back my apology—you deserve all I said and more!'

'Regan, don't be a fool. Come back here.'

Ignoring his command, she continued her wild rush along the river bank, not knowing or caring where she went as long as she put distance between herself and Bart. How dared he! How dared he flaunt his intimate knowledge of that—that woman's body to her!

Fleet of foot, and not feeling the tenderness of her soles, she sped on. It was some time before she heard the pound of Bart's boots in pursuit and when she did unreasoning panic added more speed to her flying legs. If he came near, if he touched her . . .

His hands came down heavily on her shoulders, skidding her to a halt and spinning her round to face him. Her jerk backward was an automatic reflex, as was his grab for her as her foot came down heavily on the edge of the high embankment, crumbling it to nothing. Alarm shot across his sweat-streaked face when he realised that her balance had gone, and his arms slid quickly round her to pull her closer.

Swift though the movement was, it was not swift enough and the next moment saw them both, locked in each other's arms, roll over and over, down and down, until a large boot dug into the sandbar and stopped them at the edge of the river.

Regan, winded, lay immobile for long moments, her eyes closed. Then Bart's voice sounded close to her ear.

'Are you all right?—Regan?'

The reason for her breathlessness became clear when she realised that his full weight lay over her, pressing her body into the sand.

'I will be when you get up off me!' she said distinctly without opening her eyes.

'No,' he said slowly, 'I don't think I'm going to do that yet . . . not until I've told you some more about Laura.'

Now her lids flew open wide, repudiation of whatever he might say already adding sparkle to the light sherry of her eyes.

'I don't want to hear any more about her.'

She turned her face away from his and his weight lessened slightly when he leaned on one elbow and lifted his other hand to jerk her chin back again.

'You're going to listen whether you want to or not.' A smile twisted his lips but remained clear of his eyes. 'For once I've got you in a position where you can hardly refuse.' He frowned. 'First of all I'm going to tell you that Laura is the daughter of some very good friends of mine. She's utterly delightful, enchanting, she adores me and I her—and she's three years old.'

'Three?' Regan repeated faintly, her eyes fixed on his.

'Three,' he confirmed firmly. 'She divides the time of my visits there equally between telling me she's going to marry me when she grows up, and asking me when I'm going to bring my little girl to play with her.'

Regan's head moved negatively from side to side, her eyes closing on regretful tears but still they squeezed from under her lids. 'No . . . oh no, I couldn't have——'

'Misjudged me again?' he finished grimly. 'I thought you'd know—guess—that I was talking about a child.' His voice charged with fierceness, he added: 'Do you think I'd tell *you* if there was such a woman as you imagined?'

'No,' she whispered meekly, lifting her eyes to look at him with drowning brown orbs. 'Bart . . . please. My face . . .'

She had wanted him to release her arms so that she could wipe away the tears lying on her cheeks like dewdrops. Instead, his head bent and he kissed, licked, the tears away with such tenderness that more formed in her eyes. Slowly he pulled back to stare at her, as if he had only begun to recognise the yielding yet taut contours of her body beneath the forceful maleness of his.

The sudden tremor that shook his lean frame was matched by the ripple of growing excitement shivering across her skin. Her eyes were trapped in the darkened green of his where yellow-gold motes were reflected brilliantly in the light thrown up by the sun dancing on water beside them. The river's rush over rocks worn smooth by its progress faded to a gentle background murmur while they lay as if imprisoned in a permanent tableau.

His lips moved and she drew her eyes with difficulty down to where perspiration dotted his upper lip, noting the well marked outline of his mouth and knowing that he would kiss her presently . . . make love to her with all the passion she felt mounting in his man's body melded close to hers.

Fear held no part in the emotions seeping over her. She had seen the same kind of desire in other men's eyes and been scared of its implications . . . not now.

In an unconscious gesture of provocation and submission, her chin lifted slightly to present trembling lips for him to take and do what he would with them. Never had she been so conscious of her femininity, of the basic wanton streak that overwhelmed her now with its intensity . . .

'Regan,' he groaned, like a man fighting a losing battle for control. 'Oh God, Regan . . .'

Burning, searing, his mouth closed over hers and crushed its silken softness as if he sought to master her, subdue her to his will. An unnecessary ploy at first, for Regan was quiescent, accepting, drowning in the heady pleasure of gauging the depth of her woman's power to stir him. Slowly her half slumbering passion woke to assert itself, and she returned his kisses with instinctive, unlearned skill, caressing his body with the same seeking persuasion his hands sought to apply on hers.

'Bart . . . oh, Bart!' The murmurs rose from her throat when his mouth left hers and travelled with passionate swiftness over the soft curve of her cheek to her ear, where it lingered and sent waves of primitive longing through her sensitised nerve ends. Without knowing what she pleaded for, she moaned: 'Oh, please ... please,' when his lips moved across her shoulder and down to the open front of her shirt, finding with deadly accuracy the hard tip of her breast ...

Bart's head jerked up, his eyes searching the embankment above long seconds before Regan heard the crackle of dried twigs that indicated the arrival of another being on the scene. Her dimmed vision was filled with Bart's face, white and strained, lifted alertly, his attention already withdrawn. Nonetheless, his hand moved in an automatic gesture to draw her shirt back into position.

'Oh, gee, I'm sorry,' came a vaguely familiar voice from above. 'I thought—that is, I saw somebody falling from the other side upstream, and ...'

With remarkable aplomb, and fitting his words into the quickened tempo of his breathing, Bart said: 'My wife slipped and fell, but she's all right. No broken bones.'

Regan turned her head and slowly focussed her eyes on the sturdy shorts-clad figure above them, uniform and insignia proclaiming his authority over the boys in his care. The scout leader.

'Well,' he said, his face pink from sun and embarrassment, 'if you're sure there's nothing I can do——'

'I think I can cope,' Bart returned with a trace of dryness that made Regan want to giggle suddenly. That the man from Down Under could 'cope' was the understatement of the year! 'Thanks for your concern, anyway.'

To her disappointment, Bart rolled away from her as soon as the other man had disappeared again into the undergrowth lining the bank. His silence as he sat on the coarse sand, elbows supported on raised knees, sent a cold shiver through her despite the increasing heat of the sun.

'Bart?' she said tentatively, reaching out with her hand to touch the warm bronze of his arm and flinching when he threw it off and turned to her with an angry frown.

'Leave it be, Regan,' he said, his voice raggedly impatient. 'What—happened just now shouldn't have happened. Do us both a favour and forget it, will you?'

'F-forget? How can I forget?' she stammered, then added softly, filled with wonder at her own ability to admit it at last: 'I love you, Bart. I think I always——'

'You don't love me,' he interrupted irritably. 'Why do women have to make such a thing out of a casual kiss?'

'A c-casual——?' Her breath escaped in a disbelieving gasp. How could he call what had just transpired between them a 'casual kiss'? It had moved the earth for her, and it had required very little instinctive knowledge on her part to sense that he had been equally moved. If that scoutmaster hadn't put in an untimely appearance—or was it timely? Storm clouds gathered on her brow as Bart went on again, his voice controlled and impersonal.

'That's what it was, something casual, something that happens all the time between a man and a woman without either of them weaving romantic fantasies round it.'

Regan scrambled to her feet and glared down at his bent head, ignoring the glinting silver band where the sun struck off it.

'How right you are,' she scorned, 'and I'm glad you pointed that out, because you're the last man I'd ever want to be in love with!' His head lifted, but he centred his attention on the middle of the river where an extra large rock withstood the playful wavelets breaking round it. 'You're arrogant, and bossy, and—and I pity the woman you eventually take to wife in that infernal desert you call home, because you're cold-blooded enough to marry her just to provide an heir for all those barren arcres!'

His head swivelled round in a sharp curve, his eyes narrowed glitteringly on her, but she scarcely noticed it. She was hurrying, scrambling up the loose gravelly sand of the embankment and running again, her breath coming in great gasping sobs as she made for the campsite.

She would saddle up Ladybird and head for the summer ranch alone . . . Bart could find his own way there, and his own way to the home ranch. She herself would drive one of the jeeps out over the rough terrain to the highway and be back home before nightfall. Back with the safe familiarity of Russ and Martha. And before Bart returned to the home ranch, she would be far away in Vancouver. With any luck at all, she wouldn't have to see him again before he went back to his own country.

She had almost reached the clearing when the pounding of Bart's feet on the trail close behind her spurred her to even greater speed. The love she had confessed to him had turned to ashes in her mouth, and she knew that later she would feel the full force of humiliation in his offhand rejection of the words she had never before used to a man apart from her father.

Rounding a tree whose branches bent over the trail, Regan burst into the clearing and came to a shuddering halt close to the fire, which had lost its red glow under a layer of greyish white ash.

The loud pounding of blood in her ears as she stood with heaving breast in the middle of the clearing blocked out the sounds of Bart's arrival, but when her pulses had calmed to a more normal rhythm and she looked round to the trail, obscured by trees and shrubbery, there was no sign of his lanky body. Had he passed behind her unheard and gone straight on to collect the horses?

Perhaps, but some warning premonition prompted her to take a step or two towards the trail, and then a few more until the narrow path opened up before her.

An exclamation broke from her when she saw Bart sprawled face down on the pine-strewn trail, his arms stretched out in front of him.

She hesitated before approaching him slowly, suspiciously. Was he playing some kind of trick on her to win her sympathy and so restore a modicum of normality to their relationship?

'Bart?' she called uncertainly, and then more sharply: 'Bart!' when he made no movement.

Not until she had run forward and turned his dead weight with considerable difficulty did she know without doubt that his collapse was genuine. A deep gouge on his right forehead was bleeding copiously, running freely across his temple and darkening the fair hair to a ghastly dull red. Dazedly, she looked up and found the broken-off stub of a dead branch which he must have gone full force against.

'Bart! Oh, Bart darling . . .'

Her voice came out in a soft shocked whisper, her frantic eyes seeking signs of life in the frightening greyness of his face. She drew a harsh ragged breath. Could he be——?

Even in her mind she couldn't form the dread word, and she pulled her hair back from one ear with trembling fingers, laying her head on his chest in search of an elusive heart-beat.

At first she could hear nothing but the erratic thrum of her own heart, but then at last she caught the faint but steady beat of his. He was alive! In an access of sudden relief she lay gasping on his chest, incoherent words and phrases forming on her lips. She was unaware that she uttered them until the dearly familiar drawl came, less forcefully than usual, from above her head.

'If you carry on like this, my beautiful Regan, I'll have to start believing you meant what you said back there.'

'Oh, Bart,' she jerked up to look anxiously into his half open eyes, even now holding a gleam of amusement far back in their depths.

'Does it look that bad?' His hand rose as if to touch the wound on his forehead and Regan's shot out to grasp it and pull it back to his chest—far too easily for her peace of mind.

'It looks—pretty bad, Bart,' she reported honestly, sensing that he would prefer the truth to false reassurance. 'I'll have to bathe it to find out how deep the wound is.'

Although she tried to keep her voice level and cool, he

seemed to sense that nausea was rising from her stomach to her throat and he turned his hand, which she was still holding, palm up to curl his long fingers round hers.

'If you can help me to the camp and get me some water, I can do it myself.'

'No, I'll do it,' she offered quickly. 'Will you be all right for a minute or two till I can fix something for you to rest on?'

He acquiesced with his eyes, and Regan sped the few yards back to the clearing and over to where Bart had placed the sleeping bags after rolling them neatly. Hastily, she undid their fastenings and spread them out close to the fire, then reached quickly for two of the horse blankets, tucking them under the downy bags to make a headrest.

Before going to where Bart lay, she dumped out the contents of her saddlebag and selected the white blouse she had worn the day before. It was made of cotton and would make a reasonably absorbent pad. Tearing it indiscriminately, she wadded the strips together and soaked them in the cool run of river water.

Bart's eyes were closed when she reached him, his face more grey than ever, and she thought for a moment that he had lapsed into unconsciousness, but when he felt her kneel beside him his lids fluttered open.

'That feels good,' he murmured when she applied the pad to his wound and held it there.

'Does it hurt an awful lot?'

'Can't feel . . . much of . . . anything.'

Weak from loss of blood, he leaned heavily on Regan while she guided him back to the clearing, the twenty or so yards seeming like as many miles. When at last he was stretched out on the doubled sleeping bags, the pad he had held to the wound was saturated with the bright red of his blood.

'It won't stop bleeding,' Regan muttered fiercely, kneeling beside him and looked despairingly at the flowing stream pumping steadily from the cut when she lifted the pad.

'Then I'm afraid . . . Regan . . . there's only one thing . . . to do.'

'What?' she asked eagerly, anxious to do anything that would take away that deathly pallor from his face. 'Tell me what I can do, Bart.'

Quietly, weakly, he said: 'You'll have to stitch it.'

CHAPTER TEN

'ST-STITCH it?' Regan whispered, horrified. 'I couldn't, Bart . . . I couldn't!'

'Yes, you can.' Strength gathered in his voice and his hand reached up under her hair to clasp on her neck. 'You're stronger than you think, Regan . . . I hope I'm not wrong about that . . . my life depends on it.'

'Oh, Bart, you know I'll do anything,' she cried, 'but . . . what would I use? There's nothing . . .'

'There's the fishing line,' he insisted quietly, 'and Martha's sewing kit. You can use one of the needles from that.'

'No! No, I couldn't! Don't ask that of me, Bart, please.'

'I don't want to, Regan . . . I have to. By the time you could bring medical help, I'd be . . .'

He didn't have to finish the sentence. Regan ran a desperate hand through her hair and unconsciously gripped the wrist of his hand encircling her neck.

'All right,' she said tersely. 'Can you tell me what I have to do?'

He smiled faintly. 'Good girl.' Using as few words as possible, he instructed her on what to do and seemed to lapse into semi-consciousness while she hurried to do his bidding. She cut a short length of the extra fine nylon line directly from the light rod he had used such a short time before, then collected the sewing kit and first aid box from the canvas bag, trying to blind her memory of Bart kneeling before her tending to her wounds.

Again he rallied when she knelt beside him, the threaded needle soaking in a small amount of the disinfectant from the first aid box.

'Pour the rest into the cut,' he told her quietly.

'But——'

'Do it, Regan. And,' he caught her hand in a surprisingly strong grip, 'if I should pass out, there's something I have to tell you first.'

'Tell me later,' she returned unsteadily, lifting the bottle of red liquid, her knuckles showing white where she held it. There wasn't time, she knew, for him to say anything—not even if it was to tell her he loved her as senselessly as she loved him. Her hand tipped the bottle and his teeth clamped together suddenly, swelling the ridge of his jaw to steely hardness. Regan's own breath seemed suspended in her chest until the line of his jaw relaxed slightly.

'Do it now,' he ordered in a strained voice far removed from its normal pitch.

Obediently she lifted the needle from the pan, schooling herself to look on the closing of the gaping wound as no more than the joining of two seams together. It wasn't the man she loved lying there before her, it was the silk of a material she particularly liked. She must do a good job of seaming it.

And strangely she did. A calmness descended on her, and her fingers moved neatly and methodically as she drew the edges of the wound together. The only time she faltered was when Bart groaned agonisedly and went limp, but not even that deterred her from finishing the job she had started.

It was later, after she had given a cursory glance of satisfaction at the neatly closed cut and stirred the embers of the fire into life in order to boil up the tea she was sure he would want when he came round, that she shook in every fibre of her slender being. Sitting on the fireside log and hugging her knees to still her trembling, she had to force her mind away from the horror of what she had just done. She wondered if surgeons felt like this after their first operation, and decided not. They wouldn't be operating on someone close to them, someone whose continued existence was more important than their own.

'Regan?'

'I'm here, Bart.' She rose shakily and dropped to her knees beside him, seeing the dazed greenness in his eyes.

'It's over?' he asked faintly, 'you did it?'

'I did it,' she said flippantly in reaction to the previous stress that had touched depths she had been unaware of until now. 'You're sewn up neater than a mail bag.'

Bart's jaw grew taut again, but unsure this time for the reason for it, Regan rose to her feet.

'Your tea's ready,' she said gaily. 'I thought you'd need some of the vile brew when you came to.'

'Tea?'

'Yes. I'm getting to be quite an expert, don't you think? Maybe you'll take me on as teamaker on your station if I ever come to Australia.'

'Jillaroo.'

'What?'

'You'd be a jillaroo if you came to Rowanlee as teamaker. The boys would love it, but I don't think I could permit——'

'You're not in a position to permit or not permit right now,' she reminded him pertly. 'I'll pour your tea.'

When she turned back from the fire, metal cup in hand, he appeared to have lapsed into semi-consciousness again and she knelt to look appraisingly over his face, which had better colour now that his life's blood was no longer seeping away.

'Bart? Drink this, Bart, and swallow these aspirins. Come on, wake up!'

He roused then, smiling with faint wryness as he said: 'You're out of your skull if you think . . . aspirin can cure what's ailing me.'

'Does it hurt a lot?' she asked anxiously.

'Not . . . half as much as the ache you . . . left me with on the riverbank!'

Despite the circumstances, Regan's cheeks filled with colour. Men ached, she knew, from unfulfilled erotic desire, and Bart was admitting now that his arousal had been as full and encompassing as hers had been.

'Drink your tea,' she said crisply, holding the rim of the cup to his lips and seeing him swallow with unusual meekness. He must be ill! 'Now these.' One by one she held out three aspirins, and again he swallowed them obediently. 'I've got to leave you now, Bart, but I'll be back with help within three hours. Will you be okay?'

His eyes fluttered open, 'I'll be okay, Regan. But'—his hand sought hers and held to it—'there's . . . something I . . . have to tell you.'

He sounded so vague, so apart from what was going on, that Regan squeezed his hand as if it were a child's and said: 'You can tell me later, sweetie. I have to go now.'

She looked back once after picking up Ladybird's saddle and found the sight of his virile figure reduced to baby helplessness too much to bear.

The ride on Ladybird to the summer ranch, via a short cut over the undulating hills, was a nightmare Regan blocked out of her mind for ever after. The gallant little mare, unused to being spurred on to ever greater lung-expanding power, was flagging visibly by the time the outer corrals of the summer ranch came into view. Regan hardly noticed the sleek flanks of the crossbreed Bart had come to see grazing in the enclosed pastures they flew past.

'Regan!'

Jesse Morrison, the grizzled-haired ranch boss, came out from the small squat bungalow as Regan rode up and reined Ladybird to a halt. She slid thankfully from the mare's back and half ran to the low steps where the manager stood.

'Jesse, I'm so glad you're here,' she gasped. 'There's been an——'

'I know all about it,' he chortled, holding up a calloused hand to halt her tumbling speech.

'You do?' she asked, amazed.

'Russ has just been on the radio, said you'd be coming in later today.'

Regan stared at him in bewilderment. 'Russ? Why should he——?'

'Your dad's going to be okay, Regan,' he told her with the air of a man unable to contain joyful news any longer. 'His operation went off just fine, and he's——'

'Dad? Operation? What are you talking about, Jesse?'

He stared at her uncomprehendingly, his leathery skin tinged red with embarrassment. 'You mean you didn't know? About your dad's open-heart surgery? Hell, Regan, Russ told me to be sure to let you know the minute you got here that the operation was a success . . . I thought for sure you'd know about it.'

'No, I . . .' Her legs felt suddenly weak and she leaned against the white porch pillar behind her. Useless, fragmentary thoughts tumbled slowly in her head. Dad had had open-heart surgery? Without her knowing? Hurt surged through her . . . Russ had known, Jesse obviously knew, even Bart must have known. Bart! She straightened up from the pillar, all her thoughts concentrated on Bart again.

'Jesse, I need help. The man I was with, Bart Kingman, had an accident.'

'Oh, yeah,' he drawled, 'Russ mentioned something about a cousin you were with.' His nut-brown eyes sharpened, he asked: 'What kind of accident? How bad?'

'Pretty bad,' she returned soberly. 'He ran into a tree branch and split his head open. I've stitched it up——'

'*You* stitched it?' Jesse ejaculated, looking his amazement.

'Yes,' she said hurriedly, 'but he needs a doctor. Is there any way we can reach him by pick-up?'

Swiftly she outlined the general area where she had left Bart.

'I know where you mean,' Jesse said thoughtfully, stroking his chin which was covered by a day's bristly growth. 'We should be able to get to him.'

'How long since you talked to Russ?' she asked urgently, one foot already on the porch.

'Five minutes, no more. He should still be there if you want to reach him.' Jesse half turned away. 'Don't you worry about your cousin, Regan, we'll find him okay.'

'I'm coming with you,' she said sharply. 'And I want some kind of cot fixed up in the back of the pick-up, something to cushion the bumps when we bring him in.'

The ranch boss turned to face her, one greying eyebrow lifting quizzically. 'This cousin—he's pretty important to you, huh?'

'Yes.'

'Okay, honey, we'll bring him in.'

Three minutes later Regan was talking to an incredulous Russ.

'How in hell did that happen?' he demanded, referring to Bart's accident.

'I can't go into details now, Russ, there isn't time. We're just leaving to pick him up. Can you arrange transport from your end?'

There was a pause, then Russ said doubtfully: 'I guess I could get a helicopter if it's absolutely necessary.'

'It is,' Regan said with a briefness that seemed to convince him.

'All right, I'll see to it. And Regan——?'

'What?' she asked impatiently.

'You haven't even mentioned Dad and the operation.'

Regan felt a sudden urge to breathe fire across the miles into Russ's ear.

'Since nobody thought it fit information for my ears——,' she began furiously when Russ interrupted her.

'That's the way Dad wanted it. He asked Bart to take you on the camping trip so that——'

'So that I wouldn't get in the way with my fits of girlish hysterics?' she broke in bitterly.

'Oh, come on, Regan, it was nothing like that. Dad just didn't want you worried, that's all.'

Regan softened suddenly. 'He's really all right? He's going to get better?'

Her brother's chuckle was heartening. 'I'd say so! He's already pestering them to let him transfer to a hospital nearer home. Mom says he tells them he wants to smell sage, not sea.'

The sound of a pick-up came from outside. 'I have to go now, Russ. You'll be sure to see about the helicopter?'

'Sure, Sis, I said I would, didn't I? I'll put in an emergency call right now.'

A moment later, Regan was hurrying out to the waiting truck. As promised by Jesse, a padded cot had been set up at the rear, with an added refinement of a hastily rigged canvas shade to keep the sun off the injured man. Bart.

The long jolting ride back to the summer ranch and subsequent helicopter lift to the hospital in Kamloops were for ever after a jumbled series of fleeting impressions in Regan's mind.

Bart lying as she had left him, his paleness and comatose condition striking fear into her heart. Had he already lost too much blood before her amateur stitching of the wound?

The immediate beginning of blood transfusions at the hospital, the young doctor's admiration for her emergency patchwork which, he told her, had saved Bart's life and was surprisingly neatly done.

Russ's reassuring brotherly hug on her arrival in the hospital waiting room, her own unwilling progress along the corridor to Bart's room when the doctor had relayed his wish to see Regan.

Gratitude, that was what Bart felt towards her and wanted to convey, her hesitant footsteps confirming her own unwillingness to settle for that where he was concerned. She wanted the whole bit—the gold wedding band that would bestow his name and love on her, the blond children she had pictured more than once, the adoring passion that would bring them about, the making of a home, a foundation they would build on together.

But Bart didn't want any of those things—not with her,

anyway. That much he had made clear earlier that day at the riverside. It was small comfort to know that she appealed to him physically. Earthy attraction alone was notoriously shortlived, and Regan couldn't bear her own love to grow while the man she loved grew increasingly indifferent to her as a person.

Nothing had changed, she decided with a sigh, because of the amateur operation she had performed on Bart that morning. It was best that she keep to her original intention and go to Vancouver until he left the country. She was too weary, too bruised physically and emotionally, to give a thought to the girl who might await him in his own country, the girl who probably loved it as much as he did.

A trim-figured nurse in cap and whites was holding the door of Bart's room open while she said something in a laughing tone back into the dimmed interior. That she, too, was taken by the tall blond Australian was evident in her disparaging glance over Regan's hair and clothes as she stepped past her into the room. Nothing to worry about there, she was obviously saying to herself as she went out and closed the door.

Conscious suddenly of her bedraggled appearance, Regan approached the bed, then gave an inner shrug. What did it matter anyway? She wasn't important to Bart in any meaningful way.

Despite the filtered light coming through slatted blinds, it was evident that Bart's normal healthy colour had almost returned to his face, and Regan thought she could discern an added depth to his eyes as she came to rest at the foot of the bed. Gratitude, she thought dully.

'I don't bite at close range,' the familiar drawl came, and Regan felt unexpected tears prick the back of her eyes. How near he had come to never uttering that drawl again!

'I—I'm not very good at hospital visiting,' she said, her throat dry, but she moved up closer to where his broad chest was swathed in a hospital gown, its whiteness startling against the dark bronze of his skin. She seemed numb to the effect of his lifting a long masculine hand to clasp round hers.

'But you're great at amateur surgery,' he said softly, the depth increasing in his eyes. 'The doctor said it hardly needed re-stitching, that you should be a doctor.'

'Maybe that's what I'll be, a doctor.'

His mouth quirked up in a smile. 'You'd never reach first-year exams. Some young—*lucky*—doctor would snap you up before you had a chance to open the medical books.'

No use pretending that his easygoing acceptance of her attractiveness to other men didn't hurt. It did, piercing the deadened outer layers of her feelings and probing the tenderness beneath with relentless fingers.

With great effort, she quipped: 'Then he'd have to learn that I'm a career girl and set me down twice as fast!'

His head shook slowly from side to side. 'A career girl—you? Never. You were born to be loved and taken care of by men, Regan. Your husband will simply take over from your father.'

There was a pregnant pause, during which his fingers tightened on hers. It had seemed too much of an effort to disengage her hand.

'How is your dad?'

'The—operation was a success.'

'That's good.'

'Why didn't you tell me, Bart?' she asked, her voice low and bitter. 'I'd never have gone with you on the camping trip if I'd known.'

'That was the generally accepted consensus of opinion,' he said drily, releasing her hand abruptly.

'You didn't want me to go with you anyway, did you?'

'No,' he said tightly after a pause. 'I thought you ought to be told the full facts about your father's operation and his chances of surviving it, but I was a minority of one. Everyone else, your father particularly, thought you wouldn't be able to take the possibility of his not coming through the operation. I told them that you were stronger than they thought, that you didn't need that kind of protection.' Her hand still lay on the white coverlet and he took it in his again. 'What happened this morning proved my point more than anything else could have.'

Sensing that he was about to add his thanks for saving his life, Regan withdrew her hand hastily and took a step backward.

'I—I have to go now, Bart. Russ is driving back home and I mean to sleep till morning.'

'They say it'll be a day or two before they'll let me leave here,' he said in a tone that conveyed his opinion of that stupidity. 'Will you come and see me again when you're rested?'

'No. No, I—I think I'll take off for the city as soon as possible. I—want to see for myself that Dad's okay.' A smile forced its way to her lips. 'It's possible I won't see you again before you go back to Australia.'

'You're not even going to give me a chance to thank you for what you did this morning, is that it?' His jaw took on a hardness that was by now familiar to her, but the bleak look in his eyes was not.

'There's no need. I did what had to be done, what anybody else——'

'There's no other girl I know,' he said with deliberate intentness, 'who, without any kind of medical training, would have done what you did today.'

Now embarrassment flooded over her, drowning her cheeks in rosy pink and affecting her eyelids, which blinked rapidly several times in succession.

'I wasn't very happy with you at the time, remember?' she said lightly. 'Maybe I enjoyed having you in my power for those few minutes.'

Endangering the drip solution he was attached to, Bart leaned forward and captured her wrist, drawing her over and down to the pillow his head rested on.

'And you're leaving,' he said huskily, 'without even a cousinly kiss of goodbye?'

It wasn't fair, she told herself confusedly as his fingers meshed in the tangled silk of her hair and drew her towards his mobile mouth. Her lips formed in the demure shape of what she imagined a cousinly kiss to be, but he soon disposed of that in his rough parting of them with his own and the sensuous probing that reached behind the small evenness of her teeth to the sweetness beyond. Forcefully, she drew back, thankful that his mobility was curtailed by the overhead drip attachment.

'Be seeing you, Regan,' he said with a lazy smile that sobered suddenly as he added: 'Maybe you *will* come and be my jillaroo one of these days.'

'I wouldn't count on it,' she returned, straightening from the bed and marshalling her thoughts into a semblance of coherency.

He had no right to look as forlorn, as bereft, as he had when she left his room, she told herself while walking away from him down the long corridor to the waiting room. It wasn't as if he was madly in love with her. He liked kissing her, yes . . . but that was a long way from total commitment.

The apartment in Vancouver was far from the haven Regan had envisioned for herself. Day and night traffic screeched and hummed in a way she had never noticed before. Time and again she reflected nostalgically on the camping trip with Bart, where silence had reigned apart from the gentle murmur of water over rocks and the occasional nocturnal sound of an animal seeking its mate.

A human mate would be hard to find in this cacophony of sound, she reflected bitterly, pacing the deeply carpeted living room which overlooked the yacht-studded English Bay.

Her father's remarkable progress during the three weeks she had been here should more than compensate for the relatively minor discomforts of city living, she told herself, but somehow the knowledge that Bart was still at the home ranch teased and tantalised her into an almost unbearable longing to be there with him. He didn't love her . . . that was a fact she faced squarely . . . but why shouldn't she be close to him, breathe the same air as him, for just a little while longer?

The next afternoon at the hospital provided the answer to that question.

'They're transferring me on Friday,' Phil said gleefully. 'To the hospital at Kamloops. That's almost home.'

'I'm glad, Daddy,' Regan smiled, leaning across to kiss his grizzled cheek. 'You'll never be happy anywhere else, will you?'

'No, honey, I won't.' Hester having taken fifteen minutes to visit the coffee shop far below, Phil's attention was concentrated solely on Regan. 'You'll be glad to get home too, honey, won't you?'

'Yes,' she answered with an unconscious sigh. 'I've never really liked the city.'

'You've changed somehow, darling,' her father noted seriously, his eyes roving over her thinned face. 'As if you've been hurt very badly and have no one to talk to about it. Can't you tell your old dad?'

Forcing a smile, she said: 'All I can tell him is that I'm more happy than I can say that he's going to be okay from now on.'

Phil's eyes searched hers with parental prescience. 'It's something to do with Bart, isn't it? You've changed since you went on that trip with him. You're more grown-up, more mature. And I'd guess it's due to something more than your heroic action in stitching up his forehead. Are you in love with him, honey?'

'That's a state secret,' she said lightly. 'What would you say if I told you yes and that Bart's going to carry me off to Australia with him?'

'I'd be the happiest father alive,' he said simply. 'As long as I knew it was what you wanted, that he was the man for you. I like Bart,' he ended abruptly.

'Good,' Regan said briskly, rising as her mother came into the room. 'Just as long as you don't look on him as a future son-in-law.'

Phil's eyes spoke volumes, but he spoke no more on that subject, smiling with all the love in his heart when Hester came towards them, a paperback book in her hand.

'Here's the book you wanted to read, Phil,' she said, smiling in return. 'I just beat somebody else to the last copy they had on the stand.'

Regan slipped quietly from the room, knowing her presence was dear to them but not required. At least she had set her father to rights on one count ... Bart Kingman would never be related to him more closely than he was now.

'Regan, help me with the table, will you?' Hester called as Regan passed through the hall.

'Sure, Mom,' she answered, abandoning her intention to seek out Ladybird and stretch the mare's legs on the hill close to the house. There would be other days, the long golden days of fall to roam in solitary state.

In the week since she had been back at the ranch, Regan had appeared to grow thinner, if such a thing were possible. Concern was reflected in her mother's eyes as they ran over the too fine lines of Regan's figure in yellow blouse tucked into pale coffee-coloured pants.

'Is something bothering you, darling?' she asked with assumed casualness as they worked in unison on the table, following a long-ordered routine.

'Of course not,' Regan forced a light note into her voice, aware at the same time that it didn't fool her astute mother for a moment. 'What in the world could I possibly have to bother me? Dad's in a hospital near to home and getting stronger every day, Russ and Patty are announcing their engagement as soon as Dad's home, and—well,' she shrugged, 'what do I have to bother me?'

Hester walked from the buffet with two sets of silver salt and pepper shakers, placing them conveniently at either end of the large oval table.

'I thought there might be something more personal,' she said quietly, leaning with both hands on the claret-coloured cloth. 'You've been unusually quiet since . . . well, since you went on the camping trip with Bart.'

'If memory serves me right, it was about the same time Dad was taken ill again,' Regan observed drily, her hands laying cutlery with abstracted competence. 'I guess I realised then that life wasn't all a bowl of cherries—I had to grow up some time, Mom,' she ended with a wry smile.

'So suddenly, dear?' Hester said wistfully, then looked sideways at her daughter's bent head. 'Even Bart seems to have noticed——'

'Oh, Bart!' Regan flashed, her head jerking up impatiently. 'Why doesn't he go home? I'm sure they must need his expertise there a lot more than we do!'

More gently than she would have reprimanded at one time, Hester said: 'We're very grateful to Bart for staying on to help out, especially when I'm sure he *is* needed at home. His younger brother, from what I've gathered from Edna's letters, hasn't Bart's flair for management. Besides, dear,' she turned her back on Regan and went to the buffet again, 'it's only in the past few days that he's found time to go down to the summer ranch again and look at the stock. The accident——'

Abruptly, Regan broke in on her mother's voice. 'I think I'll take that ride now, Mom, if you don't need me any more here. Ladybird and I both have some cobwebs to blow away.'

'I can manage, dear,' Hester returned, but her eyes held a worried cast as she watched her daughter walk quickly from the room. Worried and extremely thoughtful . . .

Regan, too, was thoughtful as she saddled up the delighted Ladybird and headed for her favourite hill, the cobwebs she had mentioned to her mother almost tangible in her muddled brain cells.

She had wanted Bart to be gone by the time of her return to the ranch, had schooled herself to never seeing him again. Her father's transferral to the Kamloops hospital when she had been in Vancouver for three weeks had left her with no alternative but to return with him.

How much easier it would have been not to have seen his rangy figure again, the newly healed scar on his forehead a constant reminder not only of the accident but what had gone before. Safely back in Australia, he might have looked at that scar in years to come and recalled with ever-dimming memory the girl who had stitched it for him at a campsite in the British Columbia wilderness.

Breasting the hill, Regan threw back her head to let the southern breeze feather the tendrils of hair round her face, defying the tears threatening to rise from her aching throat. How lucky men were in their ability to rouse to physical passion without becoming emotionally involved! 'A casual kiss', he had called an experience that to her had moved the earth and made her want to belong to him for evermore.

She stayed up there for a long time, absorbing the soothing familiar sensations she always felt at the broad panorama of hills and valleys spread out before her, the lake glinting in silvery ripples far below to her left. But at last, with a sigh, she turned to go, catching her breath suddenly when a solitary rider came into view between two distant slopes.

Bart! She would know that relaxed yet alert seat on a horse anywhere, even from this distance. He had retraced their journey to the summer ranch, determined to examine the stock he had come to see. Had he chosen other places to camp, places that held no memories of her or the accident that could have taken his life?

It didn't matter, she told herself fiercely, digging her heels into the startled Ladybird's sides. Soon Bart would be gone, leaving her free to gather up the threads of her life and go on from there. Meanwhile, she would avoid being alone with him as she had since her return from the city.

'Russ is going to drive me in to see your father today, dear,' her mother told her at breakfast the next morning. 'Why don't you stay at home and rest up for a change? You look as if you didn't sleep well again last night.'

To Regan's discomfiture, Bart had been finishing his breakfast when she came down. Normally he ate early and was well clear of the house before she put in an appearance, but it seemed he was in no great hurry to be off this morning, although Russ had gone about his duties.

'I'm all right, Mom,' she said edgily, pouring hot black coffee for herself at the buffet and bringing it back to the table where she sat at one end opposite her mother with Bart on her left. 'Russ has more important things to do around here than I have.'

'There are a few things he wants to talk over with your father, darling,' Hester said with gentle tact. 'I'm expecting to spend most of my time there in the coffee shop myself.'

'Oh. Well, I suppose I'll have to stay home, then,' Regan said blankly, scarcely noticing when Martha came in with a handful of letters and handed one to Bart before laying the remainder beside Hester's plate.

'Oh, dear, more bills,' she sighed, leafing through them. 'They don't seem so bad when there's the odd personal letter among them, but there isn't one today.' Her expression brightened as she looked at the unopened airmail envelope beside Bart's plate. 'Go ahead and open yours, Bart, it looks a lot more interesting than any of the other mail this morning. It's from your sister, isn't it? She's very devoted to you, I know, from the number of letters she writes to you from Europe.'

Bart made no reply, but he lifted it with an almost impatient gesture and made a neat slit in it with his knife, drawing out several closely written pages.

While his eyes scanned the lines quickly, Regan lapsed

into sour thoughts of her own. Even though his sister, Vicky, was travelling with the man she was engaged to, she still evidently felt an obligation to report regularly on her movements to big brother. Would she still feel the same after her marriage? Her husband-to-be must be somewhat spineless to——

'Something wrong, Bart?' Hester interrupted her thoughts.

'No,' he returned gruffly, clearing his throat before going on. 'At least, I hope you won't feel it's so, although it's a bad time . . .'

'Bad time for what, my dear?' Hester looked at his frowning face anxiously, her fondness for her cousin's eldest child evident in her eyes.

'It seems that my mother has written and told Vicky about my mishap on the trail, and now she and the friend she's travelling with are planning on returning to Australia via Canada.'

'Well, naturally your sister must be concerned about you, Bart. Of course she and her friend must come and stay here.'

Bart looked, to put it mildly, uncomfortable, and Regan felt an unholy stab of satisfaction. She would enjoy hearing his explanation about his sister travelling in the company of a man she was not yet married to.

'I feel it would be an imposition at this time, when Phil will be coming home any day, to have Vicky and Leslie here in addition to me.'

'Les——?' Hester began faintly. 'Your sister is travelling with—a man? Alone around Europe?'

A smile, the first to curve her lips for days, formed on Regan's face. Listening to Bart's explanation was something she was going to enjoy.

Bart abruptly scattered her complacency to the winds.

'No, Leslie is a girl. In fact,' he turned fathomless green eyes directly on Regan's, 'she's by way of being my fiancée.'

Hester's eyes, too, flew to Regan, but she was oblivious to everything but the reverberations of Bart's words, the smile frozen on her mouth. '—by way of being my fiancée . . . fiancée . . .' There *was* a girl, then, one he had asked to be his wife, one who would be the mother of his blond children . . . Of course. She had been stupid not to have realised that such a man was the next best thing to being married.

The rest of the conversation flowed around her ears in brief half-hearted snatches. Hester's belatedly delighted 'Why didn't you tell us? You must have been missing her so . . .' and pieces of 'When are they——?' and 'Leslie writes they'll be here by Monday . . .'

Leslie! All those letters he had received had been from his fiancée, not his sister. Words of longing, of love, written in that small controlled script. And Bart must have answered them—just as lovingly, just as longingly?

Regan jumped to her feet and with a muttered excuse escaped to her own room. But before tears of humiliation had a chance to fall, the door behind her was thrust open, then closed with a decisive click. She knew it was Bart even before he spoke.

'Regan, listen to me. I was going to tell you about—Leslie—about how things are between her and me, but——'

Choking down the betraying tears, Regan turned to him with blazing satirical eyes. 'But it was more fun to let me make a fool of myself, to humiliate me, wasn't it?'

'Nothing was further from my mind, Regan. Please believe that.' The line of his jaw was clamped into tautness as he came close to her and grasped the soft flesh of her upper arms. His voice dropped a notch or two to huskiness. 'You're the last person in the world I'd ever want to do that to.'

'Very noble,' she mocked, pulling away from his grasp and backing up until she felt the edge of her bed against her knees. 'Pity you're not so scrupulous about two-timing your fiancée, isn't it?'

'I don't consider I've done that.' His eyes were a bleak grey green across the distance separating them.

'You kissed me, didn't you, more than once?'

'Yes.'

'And on the last occasion it would have led to more than just kissing, wouldn't it, if it hadn't been for the appearance of the dear old scoutmaster?'

'Yes.'

Feeling her knees weakening beneath her, Regan sank on to the bed, her widened eyes still fixed on Bart's. No hesitation . . . he had freely admitted that the lovemaking initiated on the riverbank was more than just the 'casual kiss' he had indicated at the time. A lot more. She shook her head dazedly.

'You really are something, you know that? You've just informed us for the first time that you have a fiancée, and now you're up here to——' She halted suddenly, her eyes narrowing in speculation. 'Why did you come up here, Bart?'

His lips seemed to move with difficulty. 'I came to ask you not to——'

'Not to what?' she flamed when he paused, and then her eyes widened. 'Not to tell your fiancée about your little sideline with me?' Her breath caught sharply in her throat as anger squeezed with vicious hands in her chest. 'You are, without doubt, the Number One heel of the year, Bart Kingman! Why should I tell that poor girl anything?' She pulled herself up violently from the bed and stood facing him, hands on boy-slim hips. 'That kind of heartbreak is nothing compared to the punishment in store for her when she marries a cold-blooded monster like you! She has every bit of my sympathy.'

While her breast still heaved with furious agitation Bart was across the room and gripping her arm with just a little less force than would be required to break it. The scar stood out lividly against his paled skin as he gritted through his strong clenched teeth: 'One day I'm going to make you eat every one of those words, and I assure you you won't find it at all pleasant!'

Regan beat down the twinges that were half fear, half

excitement, rising from the depths of her stomach, and her eyes faced his with a rebellious flare.

'One day,' she repeated softly. 'That day would have to come very soon, wouldn't it? Or are you planning on staying here indefinitely?' She shrugged. 'Not that you could be blamed for wanting to leave that godforsaken——'

'Shut up!' he interrupted furiously, his fingers gouging painfully into her tender flesh. Bruising her again, she thought with an inward sigh, and promised herself that this time she wouldn't cover them for his sake. 'You don't know what you're talking about,' he went on contemptuously. 'Rowanlee is my home and always will be. Mine and my son's, who will carry on after me.'

'Bartram Junior,' she sneered, but her eyes momentarily betrayed the painful stab that thought brought her. Another woman would be mother to that fair-haired boy with green eyes like his father's. 'Still,' she rallied, 'I don't suppose your Leslie will object to inflicting that name on her first-born son.'

Bart's eyes narrowed to a dangerous glitter. 'My wife will have to go along with that—and other things.' He released her arm suddenly, leaving her flesh numb where his hard fingers had pressed. 'If she loves me, she'll naturally want to please me . . . as I shall her.'

That hurt too, the picture of Bart exerting himself to please the mysterious Leslie. She must be some woman to have snared the mighty Bart Kingman—and yet . . .

'*If* she loves you? You mean you aren't sure? What kind of basis is that for marriage?' A flicker of hope rose in her breast, dying to extinction with his next words.

'She'll love me,' he promised grimly. 'I won't be giving her any choice about that.'

'That's your answer to everything, isn't it?' Regan taunted. 'Sheer brute force. You can't win a woman's love that way, you know.'

'Can't I?' He took a step forward and hauled her into his arms with the same brute force she had mentioned, and bent his head to hers.

For a few moments she resisted his appeal to her senses, the ones he had so newly awakened, but shock weakened her resolve and before she knew it she was melting against him, inviting the rough caress of his hands on her body, the harsh possession of her lips.

Deep waves of pleasure arched her body in an upward reach to his, tingling excitement leaping through her veins as his hands slid with forceful demand to her hips and drew her closer to his pulsing frame. Dear God, she had thought she would never again know the hard touch of his arms, the dizzy spiralling in her brain that blotted out the rest of the universe until there were just two people spinning in a vacuum of their own making.

Two people . . . two . . . Bart and Regan . . . no, something sounded wrong there . . . Bart and—*Leslie!*

Her eyes flew open when he took his mouth away and buried it beside her neck in the rich silkiness of her hair, murmuring something there, but Regan was too shaken by her thoughts to grasp it. How could he be making love to her like this when his fiancée was due to arrive in three days?

The twisting wrench she gave separated them, making Bart's arms fall to his sides, his brows forming a slow frown of surprise. She couldn't bear to look at the darkened green of his eyes, lids heavy with the passion that still coursed through him. Her limbs felt like jelly and barely held up under her as she walked to the dressing table and used its surface to lean on, her head bent so that her hair hung down beside it.

She got out, her voice low and shaky: 'You are the most despicable, low-principled man I've ever met or hope to meet!'

'Why?' he taunted from the connecting bathroom door, his voice sounding unaffected except for an edge of curtness. 'Because I proved my point?'

'Maybe you'd be better off proving it to your fiancée!

In fact, I'll help you to do just that—I'll move out of this room and she can have it while she's here. You'll probably find the easy access convenient!'

Staring down at her white knuckles clutching the edge of the dressing table, she missed the momentary hardening of his jaw and only heard his cool acceptance of her offer.

'Thanks. It would certainly be—safer.'

Regan swung round to face him, her face burning with contempt. 'And don't you ever—*ever*,' she stressed, 'touch me again, or so help me I'll make good and sure your fiancée knows just what kind of a heel she's getting for a husband!'

His mouth went white as his lips firmed, but he said no more. Spinning on his heel, he strode in the direction of his own room.

Regan still stood as if glued to the spot. Safer, he had said. Yes, it would be safer using the privacy of the connecting doors for his nocturnal visits to his fiancée. That way, no one in the Taylor family would be aware of them and their regard for him would remain as high as ever.

No one but she would know—and she'd be damned if she'd let Bart Kingman think that it mattered one way or the other to her. She would get in touch with Leo and invite him to the ranch. He had tried to use her for his own purposes, so now she would reverse that trend.

CHAPTER ELEVEN

WHATEVER else Regan had expected of Bart's fiancée, it wasn't the sleekly groomed, quietly beautiful girl who descended from the car when Bart rushed round to open the door. Long shapely legs appeared first, followed by a skirt and jacket in lime green which fitted perfectly the curves of a stunning figure. Topping it all off was a skin that apparently held a permanent tan, and a carefully controlled sweep of black hair.

She had certainly known that the woman Bart had chosen to be his wife would be no frump, but did she have to be quite this ravishing?

It wasn't until Bart ascended the porch steps with a girl on either side that Regan noticed the one who was obviously his sister, Vicky. There was the same blonde hair, cut to a medium length and worn straight, curving slightly into her neck. Her face was a feminine version of Bart's, though her eyes were light blue and no hint of the green predominating in his. She was tall, too, perhaps an inch or so taller than Regan, and her figure in a wheat-coloured pants suit was as racehorse-lean as Regan's.

Soon the hall was filled with Australian voices, interspersed with Hester's soft English accent and Russ's firm Canadian one. Vicky, laughing up at Bart after being released from a bearhug by Russ, said mischievously:

'If I'd known I had such a handsome cousin I'd have waited before getting engaged to John.'

'Well, you can take your greedy little eyes off Russ in any case,' Bart responded drily, glancing at Regan as he added: 'He's spoken for too.'

Just as he was spoken for by this lovely girl who was standing easily, familiarly, by his side? Despite her determination not to feel emotion where Bart was concerned, Regan's heart sank when she saw what a perfect couple they made standing there. Bart so fair, Leslie so dark. The perfect combination.

'Oh, Regan,' Vicky was embracing her enthusiastically, 'you're the heroine of the hour! It's a good thing this old brother of mine wasn't depending on me to stitch him up—I'm afraid he'd have had to bleed to death!'

'Me too,' Leslie put in as she shook hands with Regan and gave her a dazzling smile that reached from white even teeth to warm dark brown eyes. 'I think you're very courageous to have done what you did for Bart.' The look she cast up at Bart was almost shy, as if she was only now becoming aware of his overpowering maleness after a prolonged separation.

'You'd have done the same as I did, given the same circumstances,' Regan returned, sounding so abrupt that Hester stepped quickly into the breach and suggested they move into the living room.

'I'll help you with the luggage,' Russ told Bart, and the two men disappeared as the women moved away.

Regan felt at a disadvantage in the faded blue denims and red checked shirt she had worn in defiance of her mother's strict injunction to wear something pretty. It had seemed important earlier that Bart should in no way think she was setting herself up in competition with his soon-to-arrive fiancée, but even a cotton dress would have given her more confidence now as she followed the well-dressed Leslie and Vicky into the living room.

Her eyes seemed irresistibly drawn to the dark girl who chatted and smiled so easily to her mother and herself. This was the woman Bart loved, the one who would be his wife, the mother of his children.

Russ appeared in the doorway, expensive-looking cases in each hand. 'Which rooms do the girls have, Mom?'

'Well, Vicky is next to you, and Leslie in Regan's room.'

'Ah-ha!' he chuckled mysteriously, turning his twinkling

eyes on Bart who, similarly laden, had come up behind him. 'How did you con Regan into agreeing to that little arrangement? She's never been known to give up her room to any other living person.'

For a brief moment Bart's eyes met Regan's, then he said smoothly: 'It was Regan's suggestion, as a matter of fact. She thought it would be more—convenient.'

'I'll say it's convenient,' Russ winked at Leslie. 'All those connecting doors and no one any the wiser.'

To Regan's surprise, a dull red flush spread under Leslie's skin, and something told her that the other girl didn't care for that kind of arrangement at all. Strange. Did her shyness extend to frigidity? Hardly possible. Not with those sultry good looks and the passionate mouth that would be any man's dream of sensuality.

Hester, who had not been at all pleased with Regan's rearrangement of the sleeping accommodation, put in: 'Russ, you're embarrassing our guest, not to mention Bart. I don't know how you could suggest——'

'I'm only joking, Mom, and I'm sorry, Leslie, if I've embarrassed you. I guess I was thinking of the temptation if Patty was next door to me.'

'We'll make very sure she never is until you're safely married, then, if that's the way your mind works,' Hester said tartly.

'It's not my mind I'm worried about,' grinned Russ irrepressibly, ignoring his mother's outraged gasp to add: 'Anyway, Regan's not as altruistic as she'd have us believe. She's very craftily moved herself into the room next to her boy-friend.'

'Let's get these cases upstairs,' Bart put in impatiently, leading the way. Angry because Russ had embarrassed his beloved?—if it was anger that caused his sudden frown, Regan mused, it must be caused by having his intentions exposed by Russ.

Vicky laughed lightly when the men had disappeared. 'I'm sure Russ didn't mean anything by his remarks, Aunt

Hester. After all, if it's Regan's room, you must have trusted Bart enough to——'

'Of course I trust Bart,' Hester said, appalled. 'He's a perfect gentleman. If I hadn't thought so, I would never have sent Regan on the camping trip alone with him.'

Regan's eyes suddenly met Leslie's, and she felt a touch of alarm when the other girl looked speculatively at her. Did she suspect the scenes that had taken place on that camping trip? Or the others that had made Regan fall so heavily for Bart? Surely, as his fiancée, Leslie knew the power of his male attraction? Perhaps even known the full extent of his passion. These days, an engagement was looked on as a minimarriage by many people. By the time the ceremony came along, they already knew all there was to know about each other.

Pain constricted her throat as she rose and murmured an excuse about dressing for dinner.

'While you're going up, dear,' Hester said, 'maybe you'll show Vicky and Leslie to their rooms. I'm sure they'd like to wash up after their journey.'

The two girls followed Regan up the broad staircase, their remarks fulsome on the spaciousness of the house.

'I've often wished we had an upper storey at home,' Vicky said wistfully. 'There's something nice about going upstairs to sleep.'

'You'd better make your wishes known to John, then,' Leslie laughed. 'I shouldn't think it's too difficult to find a two-storey house in Melbourne.'

'John loves Rowanlee so much I sometimes think he's planning to build a replica on a city-sized plot of land,' Vicky returned ruefully.

Regan opened the door to Vicky's bedroom and the three girls stepped inside, the two Australians exclaiming at the beautiful view of lake and hills from the huge picture window.

'What about you, Regan?' Leslie turned to ask, her smile more perfunctory this time, Regan thought. 'Is the boy-friend Russ mentioned—is it serious?'

'Leo? Well, I suppose you could say that. We've talked about marriage, but nothing's been settled yet.'

There, she told Leslie silently, your Bart is safe from my greedy little eyes, as he himself had said to Vicky in the hall below.

Leslie's dark brows frowned as if she hadn't believed Regan, but Vicky came back from the window at that moment and chipped in:

'He must think the world of you, Regan, to take off at the beginning of the week to come and see you. What does he do?'

'He—he's a plant biologist,' Regan answered briefly.

'Really?' Leslie's face had lit up with a gleam of interest that was dampened slightly as she turned to Vicky. 'Just like Tom Drew in London.'

'Yes,' Vicky returned drily, adding: 'And you'd better not light up like a Christmas tree in front of Bart when you mention another man's name! You know how jealous he can be.'

Leslie blinked, the animation dying completely from her face as she turned back to Regan. 'It must be wonderful for you, having a man who travels all over the world in his job.'

'Yes. In fact, I almost went with him to Central America, but then he didn't go after all.'

'Look, you two, there's lots of time to catch up on all this girlish gossip later,' said Vicky, throwing open one of the suitcases on her bed. 'I've just got to have a shower and change, I feel as if I've been wearing these clothes for ever.'

Taking the broadside hint, Regan led Leslie along the corridor to her own room.

'You'll have the same view as Vicky from here,' she was saying as she opened the door to allow Leslie to pass in front of her. 'The bathroom you'll share with——' Her voice froze in her throat when Bart, as if to corroborate her statement, emerged from the bathroom door.

' . . with me,' he supplied smoothly. 'But I don't think

we'll clash too much, do you, darling?'

'No . . . no, I'm sure not.' Leslie advanced into the room, her expressive brown eyes fawn-like in their shyness as she glanced up at Bart. Then she turned to Regan. 'It's so kind of you to give up your room for me, Regan. Any little corner would have done for me.'

'Nonsense,' Regan said crisply, avoiding Bart's enigmatic stare. 'I'm sure you have a lot of catching up to do with Bart.' She smiled sweetly at Leslie. 'Don't get too carried away, though. Dinner's in an hour.'

She withdrew, the smile pasted on her face, and stood shaking outside the door until she heard the voices from within.

'Oh, Bart,' Leslie said in a voice broken with emotion, 'I feel so——'

'I know,' he said gently, and Regan imagined his long stride diminishing the distance between himself and the woman he loved. 'I feel the same way . . .'

Sickened, Regan forced her feet into movement and reached her room without knowing quite how she got there. 'I feel the same way,' Bart's voice echoed over and over in her brain. There was all the longing in the world in those words, all the frustrated need he had tried to assuage with her, Regan.

Dinner was, in her memory, snatches of lighthearted repartee mainly between Russ and Vicky, who teased him unmercifully about Patty, who had refused to infringe on what she had termed a 'family' dinner.

'Come on, Russ, own up. This Patty of yours doesn't really exist, does she?'

'She does indeed,' Bart inserted, smiling. 'She's a delightful girl, the kind who'll be a perfect wife. She has all the virtues a man would want in a woman.'

Just as Leslie had for him, Regan thought miserably. An instinctive feeling told her that the Australian girl was able to cook superbly, care for a home calmly and with supreme ease. For a moment she hated the gently smiling

Leslie who had all the qualities Bart admired. Apparently, she also had the ability to soothe his troubled brow, for he seemed in good humour, the lines round mouth and eyes less clearly etched. What had happened in the bedroom to make him look as if a two-ton weight had been lifted from him? Sourly, she made a guess.

Leo's arrival the following afternoon seemed anticlimactic after the exuberant reception accorded Vicky and Leslie, but Regan was grateful for the dearth of other company when she greeted him as he drove up to the ranch. Vicky had gone with Russ and Hester to visit Phil, and Leslie, svelte in beige shirt and pants, had ridden out early in the day with Bart, two of Martha's packed lunches strapped to his saddle.

'What's all this about, Regan?' Leo asked, handsome in dark sweater and off-white pants as they ascended the porch steps together. 'Usually when a girl says "you owe me" I run a thousand miles in the other direction!'

'I'm sorry, Leo,' she said contritely. 'It's something I wouldn't ordinarily do, but . . .'

'Things are desperate, honey, is that it?' His arm reached round her waist, and Regan subsided into it thankfully. Whatever his faults might have been in the past, she forgave them all in that moment. She so badly needed his light-hearted admiration now!

She poured him a drink in the living room and sketchily outlined what she wanted him to do while he sat nonchalantly in one of the high-backed chairs near the window.

'So I'm to be your stooge?' he put in after a short silence.

'It sounds awful put like that, but——'

'But you're in love with this guy, huh? And I'm to act like the doting swain when he's around?'

Regan nodded twice in answer to his questions, misgivings assailing her. It was too much to ask of any man, even one who had cared so little for the things that were important to her.

'That shouldn't be too difficult,' he said quietly. 'I'd still like to be your doting swain in real life.'

'Oh, I wish I hadn't asked you to come!' Regan said miserably. 'There's just no way——'

'Don't worry, I know that. Just don't come the "one day you'll meet the right girl for you" routine—I get enough of that from my mother and sisters.' He smiled ruefully. 'All right, honey, I'll do it. This guy must have rocks in his head—though you say he's engaged to another girl?'

'Yes.'

'And you're giving him up without a struggle? Doesn't sound like you, Regan.'

'I've grown up a little since I saw you last.' She changed to another tack. 'You lost the Central American job because of me, didn't you?'

He shrugged. 'There'll be other jobs just as good. I should have realised that when it came to the crunch you weren't the type to give me the pleasure of your company without a neatly folded scrap of paper telling me I was entitled.'

Regan flushed, and he looked down into his glass with untoward seriousness. 'Maybe when this is all over, you'll consider me again. I mean,' he elaborated quickly, looking up into her eyes, 'the something borrowed, something blue bit. Marriage.'

'Oh, Leo!' Overcome with a tender rush of feeling, Regan went over to him and bent to plant a kiss in the region of his ear.

'Oops! Sorry, Regan, I can see we're interrupting a fraught moment,' Leslie's light voice came from the doorway and Regan straightened abruptly, whirling round to see Leslie's stricken face and Bart's irritated scowl behind her.

'It's all right,' she forced her voice to one of quiet friendliness, 'come in and meet Leo Shepherd.'

In one way, Leo's visit was a resounding success. The two Australian girls accepted him as Regan's boy-friend as a matter of course, and even Hester was won over by his unfailing charm in her direction. Only Russ and Bart seemed cool towards him, probably because of his earlier efforts to entice Regan away to what they regarded as a life of sin in Central America.

And that, Regan reminded herself tartly, was tantamount to Bart's old billycan calling a campfire saucepan black as far as he was concerned! At least Leo hadn't had a fiancée tucked away in the background!

Regan had found herself jealously watching the engaged couple for the signs which she knew would drive shafts of pain deep down into her, but they were few and far between. A casual male arm lightly circling a small female waist as they went out to the porch for coffee after dinner, a laugh shared by just the two of them, the interminable talking the two of them did—what did they find to talk about so intimately? Australians must, as she had originally suspected, be extremely undemonstrative in public. Unlike Russ and Patty, who could be discovered in any corner of the house wrapped blissfully in each other's arms. Of course, she sighed, Bart and Leslie had the ultimate privacy of connecting rooms. Who could ever know what went on during the long night hours?

Leo played his part to perfection, so much so that Regan almost wished that Bart had never come to Canada, that she had never known what it was to love a man completely, entirely, with a love that saw his faults and accepted them. Perhaps, once he had left the ranch, she would forget in time.

When Leo left on Friday she stood by the car talking to him, strangely sad that he would no longer be there to act as a buffer between her and everyone else collected at the ranch.

'I'm going to miss you, Leo,' she sighed. 'Do you really have to go back today?'

'I certainly do if I don't want to miss that job interview tomorrow.' His hands lifted to her shoulders as he smiled wryly. 'And I sure wish you meant that—about missing me.'

'But I will, truly. I—I don't know how I'd have survived these three days without you.'

'They've been pretty special to me, too—but it's still him, isn't it?'

She nodded. 'For now, but—I'll get over it once he leaves.'

Leo's brow wrinkled thoughfully. 'For a minute or two there last night I wondered—you know, when you and I were on the porch and he came in and switched the light on? I could have sworn he was jealous as hell because I was standing there in the moonlight with you. On the other hand,' he laughed lightly, 'it could have been his usual brotherly frown of disapproval he's displayed whenever I'm around—very similar to Russ's at times.'

'It was brotherly,' Regan said with finality, and lifted her arms to hug him. 'You'd better go, Leo, or you'll be late getting home. Give my love to everybody, and tell them I'll be coming up to the city for a week or two when Dad's on his feet again.'

'I'll look forward to it,' he said huskily, and bent to kiss her lips, more lingeringly than she was prepared for. Colour ran up under her cheeks as he got into the car and sped off along the drive. How she wished . . .

Sighing, she turned and ran up the porch steps, her eyes misted with regretful tears so that she collided with a figure standing at the top. As soon as the hard arms encircled her, she knew that they were Bart's.

'Boy-friend get away all right?' he asked casually enough, though his sharp green gaze seemed to take in the tears shimmering in her eyes.

'Yes, thanks. He—he'll be coming back as soon as he can get away again. And I'll be spending some time in Vancouver as soon as Dad's well enough to leave.' She pulled away from his arms, although her own trembled with the force of her desire to stay there and lay her head on the broad expanse of his light brown shirt. 'Excuse me, I have to do some preparing for Dad coming home this afternoon.'

'Is that why he left?—because your father's coming home?' his voice arrested her at the front door.

'Of course not. Why should you think that? It just happens that he has a job interview that could be important to him.'

'At the weekend?' The casual drawl hardened. 'Aren't most job interviews conducted during working hours?'

'Not the kind Leo's after,' she retorted, forcing herself into movement again. 'The people he has to see are mostly free only on weekends.'

Bart said nothing more, but she was conscious of his eyes on her as she crossed the hall to the stairs. Anger had already begun to simmer in her before her foot took the first step. What business was it of his as to when Leo's job interviews were conducted?

Phil's arrival home presaged the beginning of a celebratory weekend, although the sick man was confined mainly to his room, supervised by the wife who adored him and couldn't hide her pleasure in having him home again.

In consequence, the celebrations in honour of Russ's engagement to Patty were subdued and confined to a family type dinner. Vicky's irrepressible spirits, however, could make a party of any ordinary meal, and when several toasts had been drunk to the happy couple, she searched her mind for further reasons to end the bottles of champagne supplied by Bart for the occasion.

'Let me see now, we've already celebrated Bart and Leslie's engagement back home—but why shouldn't we re-celebrate it with our Canadian relatives?'

'That's enough, Vicky,' Bart snapped, his brow like thunder. 'Don't forget there's a sick man in the house.'

'She hasn't forgotten, Bart,' Leslie spoke up for his sister, her hand going to lie placatingly on Bart's arm. Her dress of lemon-coloured lace emphasised her black hair and dark eyes, and Bart's softened as he looked down into them.

'Of course she hasn't,' Hester inserted hastily. 'Phil wants everyone to enjoy the dinner. His only regret is that he's not here to join in the toasts.'

'In that case,' Vicky braved her brother's frosty gaze, 'let's toast to our homeward journey on Monday.'

From the way she raised her glass mockingly in Bart's direction, it was obvious that he too was planning to leave with Vicky and Leslie—a fact everyone but Regan seemed to have known.

'We'll miss you so much, Bart,' Hester said through a mist of sentimental tears. 'We've come to look on you as one of our own little family.'

'I have too, Aunt Hester, and I appreciate your kindness that made it so. But,' his eyes flickered very briefly over Regan's palely composed face, 'I'm needed at home now.'

'I'd sure like to see your place down there,' Russ said regretfully.

'Why don't you come, then?' Bart encompassed Patty with his smile. 'It would make a pretty good honeymoon trip.'

'Hell, man, you'll be on your own honeymoon pretty soon!' Russ interjected with a grin. 'We'll wait until the first-year storms are over in both cases.'

'Bart won't have any storms, first year or otherwise, with Leslie,' Regan put in without thinking, speaking her inner convictions impetuously, then flushing as she felt the eyes of the entire table on her. 'I mean——'

'Thank you, Regan,' Leslie said gently. 'I take that as a compliment.'

Her lovely eyes smiled across the table at Regan, who knew instantly that even if the opportunity had arisen for her to take Bart from Leslie, she couldn't have done it. The other girl's sweet serenity was a quality Bart admired in a woman, one which she herself would never have. To prove her point, as Bart would have said, a series of pictures flashed upon her inner eye. Her own defiant figure facing up to a Bart tight-jawed with fury, the kisses he had taken by way of punishment, the anger she provoked in him turning to passion in his taut body . . .

Leslie would never know him like that. With her, he would be gentle to match her gentleness, tender to match her tenderness.

'Come on, Regan,' her brother's voice broke in on her thoughts. 'Are you going to sit there all night dreaming of lover boy?'

Regan started and essayed a smile in Russ's direction. He had felt nothing but contempt for Leo, and the last visit had scarcely improved his opinion, but with brotherly affection he had made up his mind to accept the man his sister obviously cared enough for to invite him to the ranch. He had either forgotten Regan's semi-confession of being in love with Bart, or assumed that once she knew of his engagement she had put him out of her mind for good.

If only it could be that simple, she sighed, following the others from the dining room. She missed Leo's understanding of the situation; Patty, her lifelong friend, seemed on a different wavelength since she and Russ had come together. What a wonderful world it would be if hurtful areas could be cleanly excised and leave no scar.

That thought brought her eyes to Bart's forehead where the scar, so livid now, would fade to non-existence with the passage of time. He was sitting on what had become his favourite seat, the raised hearth, and his eyes lifted to meet Regan's as she came into the room. For a ridiculous moment, it seemed as if he had as much difficulty as she in breaking their locked gaze until she murmured incoherently to her mother that she would sit with Phil for a while and fled the room.

Something about that look of his puzzled her. It was familiar—so very familiar!—in its stormy anger so often directed at her. But what had she done to deserve the lash of his fury this time? She had made his fiancée welcome, and made no mention of his unfaithfulness. That, she admitted honestly as she reached her father's door, was more for Leslie's sake than for his.

'Hi, honey. You didn't have to leave the fun to come and sit with your old dad.' Phil's voice was stronger and clearer, though he seemed thinner, his face drawn.

'It's no fun for me in there, Dad,' Regan grimaced, and took the high-backed chair beside the bed.

'All engaged couples, huh? Except your mother, I guess, and she's been engaged to me for longer than either of us cares to remember!' His smile faded. 'Are you missing your young man?'

'Leo?' No.' She was suddenly tired of pretending that Leo meant something more than he did, tired of keeping up the front for everybody but her father. She had never been able to fool him for long anyway.

'It's Bart, isn't it, chicken?'

She nodded dumbly, not even bothering to brush away the heavy tears that welled from her eyes and zigzagged down her cheeks.

'And he's engaged to another girl.' Phil reached for her hand and held it tightly. 'I wish I knew what to say to comfort you, honey. All I can think of is that—another man will come along one day, one you'll love even more.'

Regan nodded again, then choked: 'Yes, I know.'

Phil's hand lifted to her face and his thumb stroked away the tears gently. 'Now I know you've really grown up,' he said huskily. 'Not too long ago you'd have said, "I don't want any other man, I want this one." And you'd have done your damnedest to take him away from a very nice girl.'

She smiled through her swimming eyes. 'You could be right, Dad. Maybe I have finally grown up.'

CHAPTER TWELVE

REGAN's new-found maturity did nothing to ease the pain of saying the final goodbye at the porch steps the following Monday morning. She had remained there after saying her farewells to Vicky and Leslie, who were now chatting with Hester and Russ beside the car.

Bart, remote and self-contained, came out of the house after saying goodbye to Phil and paused before holding out a bronzed hand to Regan. Evidently she wasn't even to receive a farewell cousinly kiss!

'H-have a safe journey home,' she murmured to the white rolled neck of his sweater.

'Thank you.' His grip tightened slightly on her hand. 'I'll never be able to forget you, Regan.'

Startled, half-hopeful, she looked up into the green eyes with their unusually serious cast, then glanced nervously at Leslie.

'Wh-what?' she stammered, meeting Bart's eyes again.

His finger indicated the scar on his forehead. 'This. Every time I look in a mirror I'll remember you and what you did for me.'

'Oh, that.' Coolly she stepped back and just as impersonally he released her hand. 'It'll fade in time.'

'Yes.' He stood looking at her for a long moment, the gold-flecked light green of his eyes darkening as they had so often when he was moved to deep emotion. Then, without giving her time to even gasp, his arms were around her and he was kissing her mouth with hard, determined lips. When he let her go, there was a faint puzzled line between his brows.

'Goodbye, my almost jillaroo,' he murmured, and turned quickly towards the car. Two minutes later it had gone, travelling at Russ's normal fast speed along the driveway to the road.

Regan's hand lifted unconsciously to touch the slight bulge under her sweater between her breasts. Already she felt comforted by the warm colours in the necklace stone Bart had brought for her. The earth and sun colours of the land he came from, the land she had so badly wanted to be part of . . .

The tears that had fallen so readily in her father's presence the night before took a long time to come to Regan that day. Blindly, instinctively, unaware of her mother's perceptive willingness to share her heartache, she saddled Ladybird and found herself some time later at the top of the hill she loved.

But today the breeze seemed to match the coldness that numbed her feelings and left her dead inside. Not even the view, when she had slid from the mare's back and dropped to the ground with her back to a tree facing the panorama of sage dotted hills and sweeping valleys, moved her.

For a long time she sat there unseeing, unfeeling, until at last thoughts began to penetrate her brain. And with the thoughts came a gradual thawing of her feelings.

Bart was gone. She would never again hear that distinctive accent, feel those hard sinewy arms around her or the hot demand of his passionate lips on hers. He would marry Leslie, beautiful Leslie who would never goad him to white-hot anger. He would know peace and tranquillity with her, live a long life in the serene home she would make for him, the children she would bear for him . . .

Now the tears flowed as if a tap had been turned on inside her somewhere. Heedlessly, she let them fall on her cheeks and drip on to the gold sweater where it curved over her breasts. It didn't matter . . . nothing mattered any more.

Nonetheless when she heard hoofbeats on the hillside behind her and the snicker of recognition between horses, she wiped her cheeks with her open palms. She didn't want

Russ to know of her foolishness in falling in love with a man who could never love her in return, even if he didn't have a beautiful fiancée.

'Did—did they get away all right?' she asked tremulously without turning.

'Well, two of them did. The other one decided he'd left a most important piece of baggage behind, one he'd never be able to manage without for the rest of his life . . .'

Regan had stiffened, not believing the evidence of her ears, but now she turned and saw the owner of that so dearly beloved drawl.

'*Bart!*' she breathed. 'Oh, Bart!'

Hardly knowing she did so, she leapt to her feet and raced into his outstretched arms. Now it was true that nothing mattered any more . . . nothing except the arms that held her, the lips that kissed her, the voice that murmured brokenly in her ear.

'How——? Why——? What——?' she questioned incoherently, her lips moving feverishly across his jaw to his eyes and back again to his mouth.

After a long and highly satisfactorily blending of lips, Bart drew slightly away. 'One question at a time, my darling,' he said huskily. 'I'll take the how first. How did I get back here? Russ brought me back when we'd seen the girls off on the plane to Vancouver.'

The girls! Regan drew in a sharp breath and pulled away from him. 'Leslie! Oh, Bart, she must have been so upset when you left her . . . just like that!'

'Would it bother you that I left her—just like that?' he asked, gently quizzing.

'Of course it would!' she cried. 'She loves you, she expects to be your *wife*! Oh, Bart, how could you have done that to her? She's a nice girl, and'—a fractional hesitation —'she's beautiful.'

His smile took her breath away as he drew her back into his arms. 'You know, Regan, that's the most *un*spoiled, *un*selfish thing I've ever heard you say.'

'But, Bart——'

He laid a finger across her lips. 'Hush and let me explain, woman! Leslie met someone else while she was in Europe—a Tom Drew, who's a plant biologist like——' His mouth tightened and he went on without mentioning Leo's name: 'Anyway, she told me about him the first day she arrived here, and *I* told *her* that that was fair dinkum because I'd fallen in love with somebody else too.'

'Me?' breathed Regan, her eyes shining up into his.

'You! Though why I should want to hitch myself to a hellcat who drives me crazy most of the time'—his hands moved sensuously over her back to her hips and he corrected—'*all* of the time, I do not know. All I do know,' his eyes grew serious, 'is that I can't live without you, Regan. I can't sleep at night for thinking about you . . . wanting you. You'll never know how much I've wanted you. That night on the trail when you kissed me in bed . . . I don't know how I kept myself from——' His voice dropped a few notches.

'And later, by the river, I'd thrown all caution to the winds and would have made love to you in the fullest way possible if that damned scoutmaster hadn't come along!'

A puzzled cast dampened the sparkle in her eyes. 'But, Bart—that's all—*physical*. That kind of love doesn't last.'

He bent to kiss her, his arms growing tight round her. 'I do care for you very much that way,' he whispered, 'but that isn't all of the game. I love your bravery, your spirit that's big enough to support your husband's when his is a bit crook, your willingness to try something you've never experienced before . . . in short,' he smiled tenderly down into her eyes, 'I love everything about you. Even the way you drive me to distraction so that I'm never sure whether to choke you or kiss you.'

Regan digested this in silence for a few moments, then said, a trace of accusation in her voice: 'You've never told me anything of this before . . . never mentioned Leslie . . .'

He sighed and looked about them. 'Let's sit down against this tree and I'll try to explain.' He led her to the tree she had leaned against and pulled her down beside him on the sun dried grass.

'Leslie was born and grew up on the property next to ours, and in the usual way our families took it for granted that one day we'd marry. It wasn't anything either of us particularly wanted, it was just the kind of thing people drift into. We're fond of each other, but more as brother and sister than lovers. Leslie realised this before I did, and wouldn't accept a ring until she'd seen something of the world, of other men.'

'I noticed she didn't wear a ring,' Regan said softly. 'I thought maybe it was a family ring that needed alteration.'

'There is a family ring,' he admitted, picking up her left hand to rub her ring finger, 'and I'd say it would fit you perfectly.'

'You haven't asked me if I want to wear it,' she said with sudden lighthearted impishness.

'I'm getting round to that,' he grinned, then sobered. 'I have to be honest and tell you that I tried to persuade Leslie in every way I could to marry me first, that we'd take a European trip as a honeymoon, but she wouldn't have it.' As if sensing Regan's quick spasm of hurt, he slid an arm round her shoulders and pulled her head to his chest. 'Thank God she didn't give in to me,' he said fervently. 'I'd never have known what it was to really love somebody, to ache for her, and know the world is just a grey nothingness without her.'

Regan lifted spontaneous lips to his, and much later mocked gently: 'And you, being you, couldn't tell one girl you loved her while another might take you up on your marriage offer.'

He smiled wryly into her upturned face. 'That's about it. It was what you said, that day at the river, that made me stop and think.'

'What I said? Bart, darling, I said so many foolish things!'

'About marrying in order to have a son to carry on at Rowanlee,' he explained seriously. 'I suddenly realised that

that was exactly why I'd wanted to marry Leslie so much. I'm thirty, there wasn't all that much time left to found a family of my own.'

'Bartram Junior,' she murmured with satisfaction.

His fingers gripped hard round her chin. 'You won't mind a narrow-shouldered, hornrimmed studious type for a son?'

'Don't be ridiculous,' she returned spiritedly. 'Our son will have blond hair and green eyes like his father, and shoulders an athlete would envy. It's all arranged.'

'Oh, sweetheart, I love you.' His breath brushed warmly against her skin before his mouth covered hers, his hands pulling her down flat beside him before they moved in a disturbing caress over her sweater. Suddenly one of the hands stopped and groped.

'Bart, what are you doing?' she asked dreamily against his lips.

'I think I'm just about to answer the "Why" of your questions,' he mumbled abstractedly, and she felt the cool breeze strike her flesh as he thrust up her sweater.

'I like what you're doing, darling,' she gurgled, 'but I can't see what it has to do with questions.'

'The reason why I came back.' He held up the gold and red stone of her necklace in triumph. 'I got to thinking on the way to the airport. Either you were growing another very misshapen and highly unnecessary protuberance, or the odd bump under your sweater I felt when I kissed you goodbye was the necklace I brought for you. In which case,' he kissed her briefly, 'it meant that Leo Shepherd didn't mean a thing to you and that I did.'

'Leo—who?' she asked in an appropriately vague murmur.

His hand curved round the slender line of her neck. 'You just be as forgetful of other men in the future, and I won't quarrel with you.'

'Sounds like a dull life you're offering me!'

A smile spread slowly over his face as he leaned over her.

'It won't be dull, that's one thing I can promise you.' He drew back a little and twisted his arm to look at his watch. 'And now I'd like a little silence while I recap on a few things before I go.'

'Go? You—you're leaving?' Regan's face fell into disappointed lines. 'But I thought——'

'I have to go, sweetheart, I really am needed at home. I can catch the afternoon plane into Vancouver and still make the early morning flight to Sydney.'

'But what about me?' she cried with a trace of her former petulant self.

'You, my darling, are going to stay here with your family until your father's better. Then, in a couple of months when I come back you'll have collected together whatever it is women collect when they marry, we'll do the deed and have our honeymoon on a leisurely trip across Australia. Then we're going to live happily ever after at Rowanlee, and have your family visit us there when we're not paying them a flying visit here.'

'Just like that, huh? It's all cut and dried—and you haven't even *asked* me yet, for heaven's sake!'

'What do you think I've been doing for the last half hour?' he said explosively, sitting up away from her and running a hand through his fair wind-tousled hair.

'A girl likes to hear it in so many words,' she quavered. 'It's something that happens to her just once in a lifetime——'

'You'd better believe it,' Bart said darkly, and pulled her up to a sitting position. 'All right, are you ready?'

A nervous giggle died in her throat when he knelt before her and looked into her eyes so deeply, so tenderly that she felt like crying instead.

'Miss Taylor, I love you with all my heart and soul, and I need you very much, and I'll do everything in my power to make you happy for the rest of our lives if you'll be mine. Will you marry me?'

'Oh, yes please, Mr Kingman,' she sighed blissfully, and willingly granted him the silence he had asked for to recap. But there was no hurry. They had the whole of their lives together ahead of them . . .

Titles available this month in the Mills & Boon ROMANCE Series

FORBIDDEN FIRE *by Charlotte Lamb*
Louise had adored her stepbrother Daniel all her young life, and now it was with a woman's love that she cared for him ....

STRANGE BEDFELLOW *by Janet Dailey*
After two years missing in the jungle, Blake Chandler had dramatically reappeared. But could his wife Dina get used to being married to this primitive stranger?

THE VELVET TOUCH *by Margery Hilton*
Laurel's first two encounters with the devastating Conde Rodrigo de Renzi of Castillo Valderosa were disastrous – but that didn't stop her falling in love with him.

LIBERATED LADY *by Sally Wentworth*
Alex Brandon plainly thought that career girl Sara was an overbearing, embittered spinster. But why should Sara care what he thought of her?

STORMY POSSESSION *by Helen Bianchin*
Marry Luke Andretti – or let her father go bankrupt. What could Sally Bellinger do but accept?

DESIRE HAS NO MERCY *by Violet Winspear*
What kind of marriage could there be between Julia and Rome Demario – she hating him, and he despising her as much as he desired her?

MAN FROM DOWN UNDER *by Elizabeth Graham*
Regan's unknown cousin Bart turned out to be handsome and forceful and she liked him very much. What a pity that he didn't like her one little bit!

LOVE'S SWEET REVENGE *by Mary Wibberley*
At last Elena was in a position to carry out her revenge on Gregor Vlados. But then she fell in love with Gregor instead ...

WALK IN THE SHADOWS *by Jayne Bauling*
To help a friend, Nicola was persuaded to pretend to be having an affair with a married man. She hadn't expected to meet the man she had been deceiving again ....

ISLE OF CALYPSO *by Margaret Rome*
Tara's plans of revenge on the aristocratic Baron Falcon Falzon went disastrously awry, and instead she found herself married to him – with all that that entailed ....

Mills & Boon Romances

– all that's pleasurable in Romantic Reading

Available March 1979

Forthcoming Mills & Boon Romances

THE SILKEN TRAP *by Charlotte Lamb*
The last thing Claire wanted was Nick Waring coming back into her life – and could she resist him now that he had?

THE MIDNIGHT SUN *by Katrina Britt*
On her honeymoon in romantic Finland, Sabina could hardly believe it when another girl turned up – and stayed, and stayed . . . .

BEHIND A CLOSED DOOR *by Jane Donnelly*
Janna found that she liked Peter Craig very much indeed – but he would never have time for any woman, except on a part-time basis. .

BRIDE FOR A NIGHT *by Anne Hampson*
Forced to marry Darius Valaris, the spirited Alida made her escape the day after the wedding. She was free of her unwanted husband – or so she thought . . . .

THE AWAKENING *by Rosemary Carter*
Robyne had disguised herself as a boy to tackle the powerful Dean Mornay – but Dean wasn't to be fooled for long . . . .

STRANGER ON THE BEACH *by Lilian Peake*
Anna was looking forward to the solitariness of the beach house – but then her unexpected, *maddening* next-door neighbour gave her a new set of problems.

WIFE IN EXCHANGE *by Robyn Donald*
Kaara's brother had run off with Don Juan de Carvallos's fiancée, and Kaara found herself forced to marry the imposing Don Juan instead!

SUN AND CANDLELIGHT *by Betty Neels*
Badly hurt by Nick Penrose, Alethea felt she could be happy with Doctor Sarre van Diederijk – but life with him was to hold a different kind of unhappiness . . . .

SUMMER RAINFALL *by Kerry Allyne*
Kim was not going to sell her farm to the local big landowner – however attractive he might be!

A VERY SPECIAL MAN *by Marjorie Lewty*
Chloe had married Benedict Dane without feeling anything 'special' for him. Now she realised that she loved him – but was it too late?

Mills & Boon Romances

– all that's pleasurable in Romantic Reading

Available April 1979